The lecherous Bret Elder's body hit the floor, and
leaped forward to give Clint a powerful hug and a passionate kiss on the mouth before he could unclench his
fists. Then, just as suddenly, she leaned back and gave
him a swat on the shoulder.

"What took you so long?" she asked breathlessly. "I
stalled him for so long I thought you weren't coming at
all."

"You're lucky the bartender at The One-Eyed Jack
knew where you were going or I wouldn't have found
you at all. Thanks for letting me know you were leaving,
by the way."

Valerie was too exhausted to say anything else. Instead, she headed for the door and stopped the instant she
looked into the saloon's main room.

Striding past her, Clint froze as well before he was
fully out of the back room. Just about every man in the
saloon had his gun out and was pointing it at Clint and
Valerie.

"That's him!" Randal Elder shouted. "A hundred dollars to whoever puts him down!"

DON'T MISS THESE
ALL-ACTION WESTERN SERIES
FROM THE BERKLEY PUBLISHING GROUP

THE GUNSMITH by J. R. Roberts
Clint Adams was a legend among lawmen, outlaws, and ladies. They called him . . . the Gunsmith.

LONGARM by Tabor Evans
The popular long-running series about Deputy U.S. Marshal Long—his life, his loves, his fight for justice.

SLOCUM by Jake Logan
Today's longest-running action Western. John Slocum rides a deadly trail of hot blood and cold steel.

BUSHWHACKERS by B. J. Lanagan
An action-packed series by the creators of Longarm! The rousing adventures of the most brutal gang of cutthroats ever assembled—Quantrill's Raiders.

DIAMONDBACK by Guy Brewer
Dex Yancey is Diamondback, a Southern gentleman turned con man when his brother cheats him out of the family fortune. Ladies love him. Gamblers hate him. But nobody pulls one over on Dex . . .

WILDGUN by Jack Hanson
The blazing adventures of mountain man Will Barlow—from the creators of Longarm!

TEXAS TRACKER by Tom Calhoun
Meet J. T. Law: the most relentless—and dangerous—man-hunter in all Texas. Where sheriffs and posses fail, he's the best man to bring in the most vicious outlaws—for a price.

THE GUNSMITH

267

NO TURNING BACK

J. R. ROBERTS

JOVE BOOKS, NEW YORK

NO TURNING BACK

A Jove Book / published by arrangement with
the author

PRINTING HISTORY
Jove edition / March 2004

For information address: The Berkley Publishing Group, a division of Penguin Group (USA) Inc., 375 Hudson Street, New York, New York 10014.

ISBN: 0-515-13699-9

A JOVE BOOK®
Jove Books are published by The Berkley Publishing Group, a division of Penguin Group (USA) Inc., 375 Hudson Street, New York, New York 10014. JOVE and the "J" design are trademarks belonging to Penguin Group (USA) Inc.

PRINTED IN THE UNITED STATES OF AMERICA

10 9 8 7 6 5 4 3 2 1

ONE

There was something truly special about the clear, California sky. No matter how many times Clint had seen it, the sight always struck a nerve deep inside of him. Coming from years of experience of sleeping in wide open spaces and seeing plenty of starry nights, he might have even considered himself an expert on such things as noticing the differences in the way the sun rose over the mountains as opposed to breaking out from behind a city.

Just as sailors used the stars and sun to guide them, so did a man who rode the open trails that crossed from one side of the United States to another. In fact, Clint thought he might have been getting sentimental in his advancing years since he'd been catching himself gazing up at the heavens more and more.

But that wasn't necessarily true. He'd just paid attention to every one of the sunrises and sunsets t'iat he'd been lucky enough to witness. The stars affected him the same way. No matter how constant they were, they somehow found a way to look different over different parts of the world. But even with all of that in mind, Clint had to admit there was something even more special about the stars in California.

Maybe they glittered a little brighter thanks to the sparkle of the ocean casting its reflected light up into the sky. Perhaps it was the wide, colorful mountain ranges or the sprawling cities that drew people's hopes as well as their wagons and bodies from as far as the opposite end of the country.

Then again, it might have just been California. Speak that word to folks from as far away as the British Isle, and they'd probably look back with a glint of gold reflected in their eyes. Whatever it was that made the place feel so different from all the rest, Clint was glad he could feel that difference. Without it, he might as well have stayed in Texas.

As it was, Clint was in his room within the Luna Hotel in Port Saunders. Port Saunders was a half day's ride south from San Francisco along the Pacific coastline. It wasn't a terribly big city, but big enough to be more than a town. Compared to San Francisco, however, Port Saunders felt calm and quaint.

It was a new moon, so the only lights in the sky were the sparkling array of stars scattered over the earth like so many discarded gemstones. The ocean was close enough for Clint to smell the salt water and if he closed his eyes and focused real hard, he could just about hear the water brushing up against the shore.

The room he'd rented was even darker than the streets below. Having put out both the lanterns, Clint sat in a chair next to an open window so he could let the night wash over him. It was summer, but the nearby ocean kept the heat from becoming unbearable. In the nighttime hours, the breeze was almost cold against his skin as it blew in through the window and under his shirt which hung open and untucked.

Although the familiar weight of his gun belt wasn't around his waist, Clint felt the worn leather holster pressed between his shoulder blade and the back of the chair. It hung over the chair right where he'd left it and close enough for him to get to just in case the need should arise.

For most men, that sort of need didn't arise too often. But Clint Adams wasn't most men. He was the Gunsmith and the path he walked took sharp and dangerous turns only too often.

While he was most definitely prepared for the worst at any given time, Clint didn't let that take away from his enjoyment of the moment. For the time being, the only things that really concerned him were the stars in front of him and the heavenly body behind his chair.

As if picking up on that thought as soon as it had crossed Clint's mind, that particular body moved through the shadows without making a sound and approached Clint from behind with arms outstretched. Fingers curled outward until they brushed over Clint's shoulders, working their way along the edge of his shirt until they found their way underneath the worn cotton.

Already reaching up to take hold of the delicate hand, Clint smiled warmly and leaned his head back as far as his neck would allow. In no time at all, he saw a familiar face descend upon him as soft lips were pressed against his mouth.

"I was trying to sneak up on you," the tall brunette with the smooth porcelain skin whispered after finishing the kiss.

Clint smirked and gave her a quick wink. "You damn near scared the hell out of me, too."

The brunette gave him a playful smack on the shoulder and dashed around to sit on Clint's lap. "Liar," she scolded. "I can't even sneak up on you when you're asleep."

"Why would I ever want to sleep when you're in my bed?"

"A man's got to catch his breath sometimes, doesn't

he? I know I sure do." When she added that second part, she seemed to be a little out of breath herself. Her eyes locked onto Clint's and her dark ruby lips parted in a sensual smile.

Clint had met Valerie just two nights before in The One-Eyed Jack, a saloon that catered strictly to serious gamblers. That didn't mean that more casual players weren't welcomed inside for a drink and a game. They just didn't last long once the professional cardsharps and sporting men sank their claws in and started fleecing them like sheep being robbed of their skins.

There hadn't been any sheep in The One-Eyed Jack since Clint had arrived in town, but that was not surprising since the gambling hall was filled with men in expensive suits sitting behind mountains of chips. Even if there had been a good amount of suckers in the place, Clint would have walked right past them and headed for the big games.

After all, it was always more fun to hook a shark instead of a guppy.

When he'd first laid eyes on the tall, slender brunette, Clint thought that she'd mistaken him for one of the unfortunate souls who wandered into The One-Eyed Jack for a casual game. In fact, she might have thought that very thing, but it wasn't long before they were enjoying nothing more than each other's company.

Winning had a similar effect on folks as whiskey and after a particularly successful night of five-card stud, Clint was on a first-name basis with the brunette. That first name was Valerie and she was rarely away from Clint's side once she'd told it to him.

Valerie had the smooth, soft body of someone born to slide naked between the sheets. Her lips were naturally the color of expensive wine and she had the voice of a natural hell-raiser. Deep and a little rough, every one of her words sounded dirty and they never failed to send a chill down Clint's spine.

This was no exception as Valerie curled up on Clint's lap and wrapped her arms around him in the dark. The only piece of clothing she wore was a sheer burgundy slip and the dim starlight that came in from the window seemed to shine right through it. Round, pink little nipples became hard in the cool breeze and she trembled slightly as Clint ran his hand along her hip and thigh.

"Think I can get you away from this window for a bit?" she asked.

"I don't know," Clint replied with a playful frown. "You tired me out pretty good. I may not be able to get my weary bones up without some help."

Valerie's hand slipped between Clint's legs. "That's fine, then. I can just see what I can do for you right here."

As the brunette lowered herself onto the floor and eased Clint's pants down, she opened her dark red lips and extended the moist tip of her tongue until she just barely touched it against his stomach. Clint let out a contented breath, ran his fingers through Valerie's hair and enjoyed the moment.

TWO

The Luna Hotel was less than half a block away from The One-Eyed Jack. Despite the fact that there were plenty of other hotels in Port Saunders, as well as some that were closer to the gambling parlor, only the Luna got as much business from the gamblers visiting the area. Part of that was because of the more comfortable beds and spacious rooms, but another contributing factor was that most of the working girls preferred that hotel over any other.

As much as the tall, well-dressed man liked to think he was a connoisseur of fine things, it was the second of those reasons that brought him over to the Luna from The One-Eyed Jack. More specifically, it was the young girl with the flowing, dark blond hair that dragged him into the hotel, giggling sexily the entire way.

"Is . . . is this where we're supposed to be going?" the man asked in a nervous British accent.

The man stood at precisely six feet tall with a stocky build. His clothes were made of tailored silk and were the color of nighttime waters, only to be offset by the glitter of a gold watch chain stretching across his stomach. Shoes polished to a shine covered his shuffling feet and a thick mane of long hair covered his face. Between the long sideburns and full beard, his mouth was barely visible. Even from what little that could be seen, however, it was obvious that he was more than a little skittish.

Guiding him along as though she was the one who outweighed him by thirty or forty pounds rather than it being the other way around, the young woman tugged his hand and all but dragged him into the hotel. Her hair hung almost to her tight little backside and was the color of straw that had spent too much time in the sun. It had a natural waviness to it that richer women would pay more than a pretty penny to duplicate.

Although thin and tall, there was nothing awkward about the woman's body or movements. Her young face was covered with a wide smile and thin red lips parted to let out an infectious laugh. "It's all right," she said. "This is the best place to go. The beds are so big, it'll give us plenty of room to—"

"That's quite all right," the man interrupted. "I . . . uh . . . get the picture."

Stopping just inside the Luna's front door, she slid her hands over the distinguished man's chest until she reached all the way up to his shoulders. "Don't be embarrassed, Martin," she said as if she'd known him for more than forty-five minutes. "Just get us a room and then you can do whatever you want. If you're a good boy, we might just do it twice."

"That sounds . . . fine. It's just that . . . uh . . . I haven't really done anything like this before," the man lied.

She didn't buy it for a second, but didn't let him know that through anything she said or did. Instead, the young woman gave him a cute smile and answered, "I'll bet you haven't. Once I get you up into that room, you'll feel all better and you won't be nervous a bit."

Martin nodded, straightened his lapels and walked over to the front desk. There was already a clerk waiting there behind the register with a pencil in hand. With the amount of business he got from The One-Eyed Jack, the clerk had his own kind of poker face which kept the customer always at ease.

"Good evening to you," the Englishman said with a curt nod.

The clerk responded with a nod of his own and handed over the pencil. "Evenin'."

"I'll need a room for the night. Preferably a suite."

"I've got just the one." As the clerk turned around to fetch a key from the row of hooks on the wall behind him, he made a mental note as to just how much the working girl's percentage would be from the cost of the room. Just to make sure everyone got what was coming to them, he also added that percentage to the real price of the suite.

The Englishman didn't so much as flinch at the adjusted price, which made the clerk sorry for not adding more. Instead, the well-dressed man wrote the name "Martin Smythe" onto the register in an ornate script before reaching for his billfold.

"This should cover the price of the room as well as whatever we might require throughout the night," Martin said after placing a few folded bills onto the counter.

The clerk was good at keeping a straight face, but not good enough to hide the glee he felt upon seeing so much money set down within his grasp. "We serve a fine breakfast and I can get you whatever you need. Just ask for me if there's anything else, Mr. Smith," the clerk gushed, mispronouncing the other man's name in his haste.

Normally a stickler for details, Martin was currently too preoccupied by the wiggle in the young girl's walk to properly correct the clerk's pronunciation.

"My name's Gus," the clerk said. "If you can't find me, just ask Addy. She'll know where to look."

"Addy?" Martin asked.

Gus gave one nod toward the young girl sauntering up

the stairs while caressing the banister as though it had paid for her time. "You are here with Addy, aren't you?"

At that moment, Martin couldn't remember if he'd even asked for the young girl's name before letting her take him to the hotel. Like any man of his standing, however, he shook off the social blunder as though it had never happened. "Of course I am. Now about that key."

Addy's trim figure was accentuated by the form-fitting dress she wore, which hugged her curves like a lover's hand. Smoothly rounded hips switched back and forth as she slowly worked her way up from one step to another. Long, slender legs peeked out occasionally from the slit in her skirt which ran up past her knees. To top it all off, she formed a sexy smile with her pouty lips the moment she knew that eyes were upon her.

Shaking his head, Gus gave the Englishman a knowing smirk which was tainted with more than a little jealousy. Making only a desk clerk's wages, he'd never been able to sample Addy's wares for himself, no matter how badly he'd wanted to every time he saw her walk up those stairs.

He was snapped out of his daydream when the key in his hand was suddenly snatched away from him by the flustered man in the expensive suit. For someone who was about to step into the promised land, Martin Smythe didn't seem too excited.

"I'll take that," Martin said as he closed his manicured fingers around the room key. "Thank you very much and I'll contact you should I require anything."

"If'n you just need a hand up there with that one, just let me know."

The lewd joke had about as much effect on Martin's disposition as water did upon a duck's back. Gus laughed all the same as he jotted down Addy's name next to the Englishman's.

Clearing his throat as though he'd been forced to swallow something vile, Smythe acknowledged the comment and turned back around to the woman who was waiting halfway up the stairs. The moment his eyes took in the sight of Addy's welcome smile and waiting body, the Englishman found his good spirits just fine.

Addy's smile widened as well. Not only was Martin a better-than-average man physically, he represented one of the better paydays that she'd had since the last prospector came to town with the last of his gold money. Even under normal circumstances, Smythe would have been a golden goose in tailored silk. But with the secret offer she'd received in addition to Martin's proposal, Addy thought she just might be able to take a much needed vacation.

When she thought about the man who'd made her that other offer regarding Martin Smythe, Addy felt a chill run through her body.

"Come on handsome," she said, hoping Martin didn't notice her momentary shudder. "It's not polite to keep a lady waiting."

THREE

Clint was still sitting in the chair next to the window. He'd scooted down a bit, allowing Valerie to settle on her knees between his legs. Leaning his head against the chair's back, Clint reached down and ran his fingers through her thick, dark hair as her lips ran up and down along the shaft of his penis.

She sucked him like he was a stick of candy, taking him all the way into her mouth one moment and then teasing him with her lips the next. All the while, she let her tongue wrap around his shaft, licking him all the way from tip to base. Every now and then, she would let him slide out of her mouth and look up at him while her tongue moved over his cock.

Before Clint had been savoring the moment, but now he tried to focus on something else for a few seconds because he didn't want the spectacular moment to come to an end. He looked into Valerie's eyes which were a dark, chocolate brown in the starlight. He looked at the almost flawless smoothness of her skin as well as the bloodred color of the lips which were about to be wrapped around him once again.

"All right," he thought. "That's not working."

Rather than make the moment last, the more Clint thought about Valerie, the more excited he became. That, combined with the way she expertly drove him into a frenzy with her lapping tongue and soft lips, only made Clint's blood burn even hotter.

She could feel the way his fingers tightened around her hair and the way his body tensed against the chair. With one hand resting on Clint's knee, Valerie slid her other hand along the base of his cock, stroking him gently as she wrapped her lips around him and went back to work. This time, she made a purring sound in the back of her throat that was partly a response to Clint's touch, but also another way to drive him crazy.

It worked.

The soft rumble of Valerie's voice was like another set of lips kissing him directly on the most sensitive part of his body. Clint took a deep breath and grabbed a handful of her hair, which only made the purring become more intense.

He could hear footsteps in the hallway outside his room. There were voices as well as another man and woman unlocked the door next to his. Although he couldn't hear exact words, Clint could tell by the sounds they made that the couple next door were quickly going to be following in his and Valerie's tracks.

Concentrating on things outside his own room helped cool Clint down just enough to pull back a bit on his own reins. Although he was still aching to jump out of his chair and toss Valerie onto the bed, he'd regained his breath and slowed his pulse down a notch or two.

With all that in mind, he let out the breath he'd been holding and looked back down at Valerie. "I'd swear you were trying to do me in," he whispered. "You're making it real hard to control myself."

"Real hard," she repeated. Sliding both hands up and down along his rigid penis, Valerie added, "I can feel that much for myself. As for the rest of it, who said I wanted you to control yourself?"

Clint reached down to take hold of her wrists and guide Valerie onto her feet. Once they were both standing in the darkness, their bodies melted together and their lips met in a passionate kiss. The longer the kiss went on, the more Valerie rubbed herself against Clint's chest and hips. She started to moan loudly as she felt his hands pull her thin slip aside and press against her naked flesh.

Without saying a word, Valerie took Clint's hand and guided it between her legs. She spread her thighs open just enough to let his fingers caress the slick lips of her vagina. A chill swept through her skin the instant his touch found the sensitive nub of her clitoris.

Clint could feel her getting wetter the more he let his fingers roam over her soft flesh. As soon as he felt her fingers once again wrapping around his cock, Clint took his hand away and let Valerie place the tip of him against her waiting lips.

All it took was a gentle push for Clint to slide inside of her. She had to grab hold of him to steady herself, but Valerie wasn't the least bit worried that Clint would let her fall. In fact, she even leaned back slightly to allow more of his length to fit inside of her. The angle was a little odd, but the reward was spectacular.

Rather than waiting to get onto the bed or even back down onto the chair, Clint was already inside of Valerie's body and they were both standing in front of an open window without a care in the world. Their passion had overwhelmed everything else until it had become so powerful that he had to get inside of her, if only just a little ways.

Valerie's leg slid over Clint's thigh, wrapping around him as she pushed her hips back and forth in time to his short thrusts. Once she had both hands locked around the back of his neck, she hopped up and into his arms while

pushing her shoulders against the window frame. It was
all Clint could do to catch her in time but once he did,
he was able to push his cock even farther into her moist
embrace.

Grinning at the surprised look on Clint's face, Valerie
squeezed her legs around him and closed her eyes. The
expression on her face was both mischievous and victorious at the same time.

"It looks like even the great Gunsmith can be rattled,"
she said.

"Maybe," Clint replied. "But not for long." With that,
he placed his hands on her smooth buttocks, lifted her up
just a little bit more and then buried himself all the way
inside of her until Valerie's eyes opened wide and a little
gasp escaped from her lips.

"Oh my God," she whispered as she felt every inch of
his length fill her up. The pleasurable shock turned into
an intense gaze as she threw all of her passion into a kiss
that damn near stole Clint's breath away.

She protested when he pulled away and tightened her
embrace as he scooped her into his arms. Clint carried
Valerie away from the wall and over to the bed where he
lowered her down until her back was resting on the mattress. Just then, something caught his attention out of the
corner of his eye. It wasn't much more than a quick flash
of light and wasn't too much brighter than some of the
more brilliant stars in the sky. What made it different was
the way it flared up and then quickly disappeared before
Clint could finish turning his head to look.

"What is it, Clint?" Valerie asked, turning to try and
see what Clint was looking at. Even though she followed
his gaze to the window, she didn't see much of anything
unusual outside. There was a quick glint that might have
been something reflecting off another pane of glass, but
that wasn't enough to keep her distracted from what Clint
was doing.

Reaching up to place a finger on Clint's chin, she asked him, "Is there something wrong?"

Valerie's heart skipped a beat when Clint's hand flashed up from the shadows and clamped down on her wrist. Rather than simply pull her hand away from his face, he kept going until he felt her arm pound against the bed. In less than a second, Clint had her other wrist as well and slammed it down against the mattress on the other side of her head.

Despite the fact that he could still see that peculiar glint in his mind's eye, Clint hadn't seen enough to pull him away from the heat warming him from Valerie's soft skin. "Wrong?" he asked, while looking back at Valerie with a sly grin on his face. "The only thing wrong is that you're still wearing that slip."

The trepidation that had been building in Valerie's mind faded quickly away as she squirmed beneath Clint's weight. "You frightened me."

"You loved it."

"Maybe," she admitted in a sultry whisper. "Just a little."

"Now, about that slip." Not letting Valerie get a moment to reply, Clint shifted so that he was holding on to both of her wrists with one hand. His other hand went down to the neckline of Valerie's slip, which was torn straight down the middle with one quick, powerful tug.

Valerie let out a shocked breath and arched her back beneath him. Her eyes were wide with genuine surprise, but she couldn't hide the arousal that flushed her cheeks and sent the blood speeding through her veins. She did struggle against Clint's grip upon her, but not nearly enough to actually free herself. Once she felt a wrist start to come out from between his thumb and fingers, she eased up to keep it right where it was.

Gazing down at Valerie's body, Clint followed the line of the rip he'd created in her thin cotton slip. The tear stopped just below her waist, exposing her small, yet firm breasts as well as the taut line of her stomach muscles. "I've been wanting to do that for a while," he said.

Even though she still seemed genuinely surprised by Clint's sudden movement and actions, Valerie couldn't hide the fact that she was more aroused than ever. The fact that her breasts were exposed after the ripping of fabric made her nipples erect and she shuddered powerfully when Clint lowered his mouth down to suck on the little pink mounds.

As he nibbled and licked her breasts, Clint ripped the slip even more until it fell open into two complete halves. He settled on top of her after Valerie opened her legs even wider for him and used his free hand to guide his cock into her wet pussy.

Pushing all the way inside of her, Clint almost forgot about that odd flicker he'd spotted through the window out of the corner of his eye. He almost forgot, but not quite.

FOUR

While the Port Arms Hotel was nowhere near as comfortable as the Luna, its prices were better suited for the men who came out on the wrong side of any of the games played at The One-Eyed Jack. Oftentimes, both establishments were used for the same purposes and frequently by the same people. The main difference was merely which way Lady Luck happened to be glancing on any particular evening.

Of course, having players look away at the wrong moment could also draw the line between those who slept at the Luna and those who stretched out on a crooked cot at the Port Arms.

For the man sitting in the dark with his chest pressed against the back of a chair, neither of those reasons explained why he was at the Port Arms when he could easily afford a suite at the place across the street. He sat straddling the chair, facing one direction while the rickety piece of furniture faced the other as though everyone else who'd used the seat had been doing it the wrong way.

Just like one of the guests at the Luna, the man across the street sat without a single light burning in his room. Unlike that other person, however, the man didn't appear to be savoring the night or even moving his eyes away from the other buildings outside his window to gaze up at something so frivolous as the stars and sky.

His muscles twitched in response to nearly every sound he heard, but not enough to show as anything else but a little flicker of motion. Each one could be the beginning of a reaction if the man decided to let himself move more than a fraction of an inch. His eyes wavered slightly when something moved nearby, but only enough for him to see what the source of his distraction was.

He was aware of everything around him, whether or not it moved or breathed. Absorbing everything he could, the man became one with his surroundings which was exactly the way he'd been trained.

Without looking closely at him, a casual observer might not even realize he was there at all. His movements were slight and nearly imperceptible. When he did turn to look in another direction or reach for something nearby, he flowed like he was slipping through water, smooth and circular.

If they could spot him sitting in the dark, that same observer would see a face that wouldn't stick in their memories for much longer than it would take to cross the street. The man appeared casually serious, yet somewhat bored at the same time. His short hair and clean-shaven features made him resemble any of a thousand other fellows ranging from small-time businessmen to faithful sons and husbands. Even if he stood up, the man's average frame filled out a suit of clothes much the same as any other body.

The differences lay in what was beneath the surface. Beneath the carefully constructed and well-maintained exterior, there was a level of darkness rivaling that of the night itself. Every so often, it could be seen in a grim set of his jaw or the intense fire burning deep in his eyes.

Not many people got to see that side of him for themselves.

Those that did see it rarely lived to spread the word.

For the moment, the man didn't want anyone to see him, so he sat perfectly still in the darkness. He surveyed the street below his window, but mainly focused on the upper floor windows of the Luna Hotel. One of those windows in particular caught his eye as a lantern came on but was quickly doused, briefly illuminating a pair of entwined bodies.

As always, it was a busy night for the Luna. More specifically, it was a busy night for the girls working The One-Eyed Jack. He'd been watching another window where he was surprised to see a woman who normally made her money working the card tables rather than the men who played at them. It was her appearance that had drawn another familiar face into the open.

The man knew Clint Adams was in town, but he didn't know that he'd been looking at the Gunsmith for close to an hour. It wasn't too surprising considering the fact that Adams was known to be something more than just a gun hand. But Gunsmith or not, the man across from the Luna wasn't going to let himself be drawn off his course.

By the looks of it, Adams wasn't going to be any concern since the woman from the gambling hall was keeping him more than a little busy. As soon as he saw Adams carry the brunette deeper into the room, the man reached for an item that had been folded up and carefully placed on his right knee.

The little round spectacles were light and made of bent copper. The lenses were thin and light enough so that the man barely felt it when he set them on the bridge of his nose and hooked the thin arms behind each ear.

Those spectacles served him two different ways. First of all, they made him appear to be even less of a threat and slightly weak when in public. Secondly, and most importantly, they shifted his sight into just slightly better focus. While most people might not have noticed the subtle difference and would have been more than happy to settle for near-perfect sight with their naked eyes, the man in the dark noticed the change very much indeed.

It allowed him to pick out minute details like when someone's eyes were looking directly at him or something next to him. It allowed him to see muscles twitch just before someone was about to move an arm or leg. It even allowed him to see another person's chest rise or fall when they were breathing in or out.

Anyone who paid enough attention could have spotted those things as well with a bit of effort and training. The man in the dark had had plenty of training and expended enough effort to wear out a bull. The glasses simply made him better.

Everything combined made him damn near perfect. Being in his line of work, the man couldn't afford to settle for anything less than that.

Moving only his left arm, the man picked up a rifle which had been leaning against the wall beneath the window. Without looking, he let his hands go through the motions of checking the weapon and preparing it to be fired.

It felt comfortable and familiar as a wife's hug when he lifted the rifle up and pressed the stock against his shoulder. He gazed through the spectacles, down the length of the barrel and centered on his target. For a moment, it had seemed that Adams was looking over at him, but he'd since disappeared into his own room.

The man didn't worry about Adams. All that mattered was the job and after a few more breaths and the squeeze of a trigger, that job would be completed.

FIVE

Addy had dealt with men like Martin Smythe before. In fact, she specialized in them. All the other girls who worked with her said that Addy was the one to crack even the toughest customer. Some men came into The One-Eyed Jack to play cards and make money and nothing else. Those were the ones that wanted to be left alone and the working girls were more than happy to oblige.

But Addy looked at men like that as a challenge. Also, once they were loosened up, they tended to pay her plenty for getting them to see the light. Addy had a way about her that was insistent but in a way that made a man miss her when she was gone. Now that she'd gotten Martin into a private suite, however, she wasn't planning on going anywhere.

"So what do you do for a living?" she asked while slowly unbuttoning Martin's shirt and pulling off his suit coat.

The Englishman seemed a bit uncomfortable, but only when his thumb grazed the gold band around his left ring finger. "I work for the British government."

Only half listening to him, Addy raised her eyebrows

and put on an impressed expression. "Oh really? That sounds important."

"I do quite a bit of traveling."

"I'll just bet you do."

Her hands had found their way under Martin's clothes and were exploring his soft, pale skin. The Englishman drew in a sharp breath and when he opened his eyes again, his belt was unbuckled, and his pants were on their way down.

"I don't . . . usually do this sort of thing," he said meekly.

Addy had not only seen the other man's wedding ring, but had taken that into consideration when approaching him at The One-Eyed Jack. Every kind of man had their triggers. Married ones were no exception. She just had to make sure she was slow and gentle at first, but moved quickly once the fun started.

"It's all right," she whispered, taking her hands off of him and peeling the top of her blouse down off her shoulders. The clothing fell away easily to expose a pair of tight, rounded breasts. She kept her hands moving until her skirt was sliding over her hips and she stood before him wearing nothing but a short, white underskirt.

With a defensive protest still on the tip of his tongue, Martin swallowed hard as his eyes drank in the sight of Addy's body. She was young and naturally beautiful, both of which she knew very well without having to be told. She lowered her head and smiled demurely as he looked at her. Then, before he could say another word, she reached out and took him by the hand.

"Come along now," she said while leading him to the bed. "I just want you to feel good. Don't you want to feel good?"

When she'd asked that last question, Addy took Martin's hand and moved it over her breasts. That was the straw that broke the English camel's back and every bit of resistance that he'd been trying to maintain fell away completely.

Even as he'd followed her to the hotel, paid for the room and unlocked the door, the Englishman had been thinking he might change his mind and turn away. Not only was he no longer weighing that option, but he doubted he could turn back now if his life depended on it. Smart enough to know when he was beaten, Martin let out the breath he'd been holding and practically split his trousers in two while trying to get out of them.

Addy's lips curled into a wide, excited smile. Just when she was starting to think that she might have trouble with this one, Martin toppled like a poorly built house of cards. The moment she put her hands on him below the waistline, she saw his eyes roll up into the back of his head, and a somewhat silly looking grin fill his face.

"That feels good," he said as Addy's fingernails traced lightly over his thighs. He wanted to say something else when her wet lips closed around his penis, but was unable to put a single word together.

After only a few strokes of her tongue against his shaft, Martin reached down as if to lift her onto the bed. Before he could get his hands upon her, however, Addy stopped him with a stern expression and a sharp wave of her finger.

"Not yet," she scolded teasingly. Slipping out of her underskirt, she pointed to the thatch of dark hair between her legs and said, "Before I feel you here, I want to feel you . . ."—her finger ran up her stomach and stopped between her breasts—". . . here."

Martin's eyes went even wider, but they closed once Addy lifted herself up high enough to run the tip of his cock over her stomach, along the same line she'd just traced with her finger. She bounced slowly using her knees and legs, pressing her breasts tightly around his penis and using their soft, warm flesh to massage his erect shaft.

Only when she saw that Martin was completely absorbed by the bliss he was feeling did Addy sneak a quick glance toward the window.

SIX

Clint crawled on top of Valerie's squirming, writhing body while keeping both hands locked tightly around her wrists. His grip grew stronger as his thrusts came deeper and faster, but Valerie was savoring every last second of it all.

Her eyes were tightly shut and her face was twisted into an expression that reflected the intense pleasure that had an even tighter hold on her than Clint did holding her wrists. She dug her heels into the mattress and arched her back as Clint's weight pressed down on top of her and his rock-hard cock drove all the way into her wet pussy.

Although she could neither reach up and wrap her arms around him like she so desperately wanted nor dig her nails into his flesh, the fact that she was deprived of those things only made her passion burn all the brighter. She knew she could take back some bit of control, but there wasn't a single part of her that wanted to do such a thing at that moment.

Clint looked down at her and let his eyes wander over the delicious curves of her wriggling body. Every time he drove into her, the muscles in her stomach and shoulders would tense and her face took on a breathless, faraway expression. The only sounds she made were cries of passion that played on him almost as well as her fingers or lips.

Keeping ahold of her hands had just been a little game at first, but it had seemed to drive Valerie to the brink of an orgasm every time she struggled and was denied movement. He'd let her go once, but her arms had stayed over her head and her hands hadn't moved from the grooves they'd worn into the mattress.

When Clint took hold of them again, he tightened his grip just a bit and pulled his cock almost completely out of her. She looked up at him as though she was going to cry, but smiled widely and threw her head back as he slid back inside of her wet lips.

Even in the scant starlight that leaked in through the window, Clint could see the sweat glistening off of Valerie's body. She worked with every muscle she had to grind against him or pump her hips in time to his constant, powerful thrusts. She tensed and relaxed so often that she didn't even have the strength left to wrap her legs around him any longer. Instead, she slid one foot along his leg and let the other leg rest on the bed, spreading them open enough to make sure Clint had plenty of room to keep pumping between them.

Clint knew how to read a woman's body. Judging by the way Valerie was breathing and by the way her muscles had moved beneath him, he knew she'd climaxed at least twice already. As if to confirm this, she opened her eyes as though she barely had enough strength to lift the lids without help. But even though she was out of strength, she urged him to go on with short, breathy commands.

Clint threw himself completely into the moment, savoring every last second of it as he pushed in and out of her, using every muscle at his command. Her vagina tightened around him and Valerie's entire body tensed when he drove deeply into her. Soon, he could feel the tide swelling within himself and kept right on thrusting until it exploded.

The release was so powerful that it made Clint's eyes clench shut and his grip around Valerie's wrists become tighter than he'd previously allowed it to get. Even though she winced a bit, she still enjoyed the feel of him taking such complete control over her and if she wasn't so completely spent, she might have felt another orgasm pulse through her flesh.

He was still hard inside of her, even after his climax had run its course. Rather than pull out, Clint loosened his grip around her wrists and stayed where he was. Valerie reached up to rub his shoulders as they both enjoyed the calm after the storm.

In the room next door, Martin Smythe was feeling the room spin crazily around him. This was due mainly to the fact that Addy still wasn't letting him get onto the bed. Rather than allow him to crawl on top of her the way every part of him ached to do, she sat on the edge of the mattress and used her mouth to taste every inch of him she could reach.

Her teeth nipped playfully at his chest and stomach as she worked her way down to his swollen penis. After glancing quickly toward the window, she opened her mouth and took him inside.

Unlike the last couple of times she'd taken those quick peeks, Martin actually spotted her doing it this most recent time. He reflexively looked in the same direction and saw nothing but the dark face of the building across the street.

"What is it?" he asked. "What were you . . ."

The rest of his question was lost when Martin felt the sudden swirling of Addy's tongue around his rigid penis. No matter how good it felt, the Englishman wanted even more to get on top of her and pump inside of her. After

all, that was the whole reason he'd agreed to the younger
woman's outrageous price.

"Lie down," he said, suddenly developing a backbone
after being led by the nose for this long.

Addy looked up at him and shook her head. "I'm not
done with you yet. Don't you want to make this last?"

"I want you to lie down and as long as I'm the one
with the money, you'll do as I say."

Sliding her hands up along the Englishman's sides, she
smiled widely and flicked her tongue along the underside
of his cock. "Just a little longer, sweetie. It'll be worth it,
don't you worry."

"I've waited quite long enough. Lie down."

"Ooo, I like it when a man gets bossy," she said as her
nails scraped along Martin's skin.

Hearing that, the Englishman raised his eyebrows and
smirked like a teenaged boy. "Really? You like that, do
you?"

She nodded and wrapped her lips around his cock,
sucking him in all the way down to the shaft.

Speaking in the best authoritative voice he could mus-
ter under the circumstances, Martin put his hands on her
head and eased her back. "You'll lie on that bed now.
I've got something to give you."

Addy stuck her lower lip out in a pout. "You sure you
don't want me to finish?"

"Quite."

This time, when she looked out the window, she saw
what she'd been waiting for. "Then just stand right there
for another second."

Martin started to ask why he should do that, but
couldn't get the words out. The only thing that did come
out was a gout of blood from his left temple followed by
a spray of bits of brain and skull. His eyes were still open,
but they seemed as vacant and glassy as windows of a
house that had just been cleared out.

It took a moment for Addy to realize that she was huddled down on the edge of the bed with both hands covering her head. Once the Englishman's body wavered a bit and then fell over, she hopped to her feet and pulled on the rest of her clothes.

She didn't bother looking out the window again, because she knew there would be nothing more to see. Instead, she bolted for the door but stopped before pulling it open. It was nothing more than reflex that made her stop, turn around, and search the dead man's pockets.

Smythe had fifty dollars in a billfold inside a jacket pocket and his belt was fat and fitted with small compartments as well. Being an expert in the field, Addy got the billfold and belt in her possession with a few quick motions and was once again headed out the door.

On her way out, she left the Englishman with one last question. "Who's got the money now, asshole?"

SEVEN

Clint heard the shot and was on his feet before Valerie had a chance to realize what was going on. She noticed that his weight was no longer on top of her first, and then she started to miss his warmth just as she saw that he'd moved like a flicker of lightning and was now pulling on his pants and shirt.

"What's going on?" she spat out while sitting bolt upright and pulling some of the blankets over her naked body. "What's the matter, Clint?"

Already dressed and tugging his boots over his feet, Clint snatched up his gun belt and buckled it around his waist. "That was a gunshot," he said as he walked over to the window. "It came from outside, but I think it was aimed in this direction."

"What? How do you know?"

"Because I heard glass breaking. Didn't you hear something drop next door?"

"I didn't exactly have my mind on what was happening next door," she said while her cheeks flushed and she started to climb down from the bed. "Can you see anything out there?"

Clint stopped her with a sharp, upraised hand. "Don't

move," he said. Pressing his shoulder against the wall beside the window, Clint only glanced through the glass using one cautious eye. "Stay down."

Although she was getting more frightened by the moment, Valerie did as she was told and dropped down until her chest was against the mattress. From there, she slid down to the floor, taking the blankets right along with her to use as cover.

As he peeked out the window, Clint thought back to that glimmer of reflected light he'd seen earlier. It could have come from one of the rooms across the street which would have been about right for where that gunshot might have come from. Of course, all of this was based on a single shot he'd heard that had come from out of nowhere.

Anyone else might have been too rattled to pay such close attention, too relaxed to be on his guard so quickly, or too rushed to be able to put much of anything together. But Clint was never too far off his guard and knew better than to rush into anything. What's more, he could tell plenty about that single shot. Lord only knew how many of them he'd heard in his lifetime.

All of that flew through Clint's mind in a rush. As it did, his eyes strained through the darkness to catch something that would shed some more light upon what had happened and where it had come from. He couldn't make out any broken panes across the street and couldn't spot any gun barrels poking out from an open window.

He did, however, catch a sliver of light which appeared, widened, shrank again and then disappeared. The main reason he saw it was because he'd been keeping most of his attention focused on that same room where he'd seen the reflected light minutes ago. The rest was simple observation.

Someone had opened and shut a door in that room he'd been watching. And since it happened right after a shot had been fired, Clint guessed that somebody was leaving rather than entering that same room. All he had to do now was keep watching for someone to walk outside the Port Arms Hotel.

Unfortunately, there was still things that needed to be done right there in the Luna.

"Valerie," Clint said. "Come on over here."

"Is it safe?"

"It should be," Clint said in a comforting tone. "Besides, nobody shot into this room, remember?"

Nodding, the brunette scooted across the floor toward Clint.

Clint reached down to put his hands on her shoulders and knelt down to her level. "Keep an eye on that hotel down there for me. I need you to look out for anyone who leaves that place. Try to remember any unfamiliar faces as well as the names of any faces you recognize. Think you can do that for me?"

"I guess, but why?"

"I think whoever fired that shot is on their way out any second. Just please do your best to remember as many of them as you can. Would you do that for me?"

She took a deep breath, nodded once more and went over to the window so she could peer down at the street below. She hardly even noticed the gentle kiss that was placed on the top of her head as a thank-you. She most definitely noticed when Clint headed for the door. "Where are you going?" she asked.

"To see who was on the receiving end of that bullet."

EIGHT

Normally, Clint wouldn't have put anyone in harm's way right after a shot had been fired. But something in his gut told him that that one shot hadn't been the beginning of an onslaught and that it hadn't even been fired in anger. If someone had fired a single shot from across the street and then left their room, they were after someone specific. More than likely, if that wasn't the case, there would have been plenty more shots fired already.

Something that Clint didn't bother explaining to Valerie was that he'd heard someone drop in the room next door, which probably meant that the marksman had found his target. Although that made him feel better that the shooting was over for the moment, Clint didn't take much comfort from the situation as a whole.

That was especially the case when he left his room just in time to see the neighboring door fly open and a figure come rushing outside.

Clint didn't have to be much on the ball to catch the person as they came charging out of the room. All he needed was a torso to stop the person and a pair of arms to keep them from going anywhere after they'd bounced off of him. Locking a tight grip around the figure, Clint squeezed just enough to push some of the wind from their sails and lifted them off the ground so their feet couldn't take them any farther.

"Let me go, dammit!" Addy screamed as she squirmed in Clint's arms. Her feet were still moving even though there was nothing but air beneath them.

Still keeping a tight hold on the young woman, Clint sidestepped so he could look at the door that was still swinging on its hinges after having been knocked against the wall. The dead body lay on the floor inside that other room, plain as day and the rush of cool air wagging the curtains was a good indicator of an open window.

Either that or a broken window.

"All right, all right," Clint said. "Where were you going in such a rush?"

"What does it matter? Just let go of me!"

"Something happen to your friend in there?"

"I don't know! Let me go!"

"Fine then," Clint said, setting her onto her feet. "Now that I got a good look at you, I can describe you to the law when they ask who killed that fellow in there."

That slowed her down real quickly. Suddenly, her feet stopped churning like paddles in a stream and her body relaxed within Clint's grasp. It was all Clint could do to pretend he felt half as calm as the woman in his arms appeared to be.

"If you run from me, I'll only be that much angrier when I catch you again," Clint warned.

"Yeah, yeah."

The resignation in her voice more than the actual words she spoke was enough for Clint to think he'd bought a few moments of quiet from the woman. He set her down on her own two feet and took his arms from around her. The young woman pulled away from him, but she didn't try bolting down the hall.

"Now what the hell happened in there?" Clint asked.

"I don't know. I was with a man and someone shot him through the window."

"Who is he?"

"Some English fella that picked me up at The One-Eyed Jack. I think his name was Martin."

"Is he dead?"

"If he ain't, he's putting on one hell of a show. Can I go now?"

Clint walked into the other room, grabbing hold of the woman's wrist as he did. She struggled with all she had, but Clint wasn't about to let her go. Not yet, anyway.

Keeping his head low, Clint entered the room cautiously. His hand floated in the vicinity of his holstered Colt, ready to draw the weapon at the first hint that it might be needed. One thing was for certain, though. He wasn't going to get any trouble from the man lying on the floor.

Sure enough, the window had a single bullet hole punched through its pane with cracks jutting out from the opening like a spider's web. The dead man was missing one side of his head as well as half his clothing. A quick glance told Clint that the man had been interrupted at one hell of a bad time. At least he died happy.

"You go through his pockets?" Clint asked, his eyes still focused on the clothing that had been pulled open and yanked inside out in places.

The woman shrugged. "Yeah. So what? He don't need any of that money anymore."

"Maybe not, but it's still a crime. Tell me everything that happened here and I might just forget about it."

"I don't know anything, I swear. Just let me go before that killer comes over here! Someone murdered a man and you're messing around with me!"

"I'm not the law," Clint said in a growling whisper. "I can mess with whoever I want. Now tell me everything so I can find someone else to mess with and leave you alone."

"Fine, fine. Jesus Christ! His name was Martin. He's English and he's some kind of important government type or something."

Clint pulled his eyes away from the corpse and the room so he could focus on the young woman's face. "Government type? You mean like an ambassador?"

"I don't know. All I know is that I was supposed to—"

In her rush to get away from Clint, Addy had said just a little more than she'd wanted. Her lips snapped shut and she quickly turned her head.

"Supposed to what?" Clint asked. "I already know you knew he was going to die. You're nowhere near rattled enough to have had something like this just drop on you from out of nowhere. You might as well say the rest or you just might not have enough time to get away before that shooter comes here to check on his handiwork."

"He was some plain-looking man I met at The One-Eyed Jack. About your height and weight. Brown hair. He paid me to get this Englishman over here and keep him by the window. That's all I know, I swear!"

Clint nodded. He believed she'd told him everything he was going to get out of her right then and there. She was finally getting fidgety enough to fit her situation.

"All right then," he said, releasing her wrist.

She was out the door and flying down the hall as though her caboose was on fire. Following closely behind her, Clint stepped into the hall and poked his head into the doorway of his own room. Valerie was crouching right where he'd left her.

"You see anyone come out of that hotel?" he asked her.

"Just a few. The owner was one of them and he's standing in the crowd in the street. Someone must have heard the shot."

"Did you see a man about my height with brown hair?"

"Yes, I did! Do you know him?"

When he'd first told her to watch the street, Clint had mainly been trying to keep Valerie out of harm's way. Now, however, it seemed that she was proving to be very valuable indeed. If that dead Englishman was any kind of important figure, this was more than a murder.

It was an assassination.

Murderers hightailed it out of their spot when they killed a man. Assassins needed to make sure they'd put their target down.

"Come on," he said while extending a hand to Valerie. "I need to get you into another room. We may be getting a visitor."

NINE

Adam Meers blended into the crowd without receiving so much as a second glance. All he had to do after firing the shot that had dropped Martin Smythe was wrap his rifle up in a blanket and carry it under his arm as he went to the window at the end of the hall. From there, he simply dropped the bundle into the alley below and joined the others who were darting through the hallway like chickens with their heads cut off.

Meers put on a well-rehearsed expression of fear and panic and proceeded to the stairs in a convincingly disorderly fashion. The Port Arms Hotel wasn't exactly filled to capacity, but there were enough other guests and workers around to provide ample cover.

The truth of the matter was that Meers could have used a group of one or two others as more than ample cover. That had all been part of his training.

Some of the guests asked him questions like did he hear the gunshot or what the hell was happening, but Meers only replied with a confused shrug or some vague sentence that didn't tell anyone much of anything except that someone had been shot and the gunman was somewhere nearby.

He also did a fine job of appearing just frightened enough to spread those words in a manner that fanned the flames that had already been stirring throughout the little crowd within the hotel. By the time he emerged from the Port Arms a few minutes later, Meers was accompanied by at least half a dozen others.

Not all of them were scared. Some just wanted to see what was going on and what all the fuss was about. Others were the morbid type who hoped to see some real blood or witness a live gunfight. Whatever their reasons, they served their primary purpose well enough, which was to leave the hotel in a group so that Meers wasn't the only one.

Although the expression on his face mimicked those around him, Meers was carefully scanning the street for any sign that someone was wiser than the company he currently kept. So far, it didn't seem like he would have a problem, but he knew better than to take that as gospel. There was still work that needed to be done.

Meers glanced toward the upper windows of the Luna Hotel. He wasn't the only one who'd spotted the broken glass, so he took his time in surveying the scene. He was more interested in the window next to the broken one. That was where he'd spotted Clint Adams. So far, there still didn't seem to be any activity or even a light burning inside that room.

The Gunsmith wasn't in the crowd yet, either, which was more good news in Meers's mind.

What little comfort he took from that quickly dissipated, however, when he saw Adams talking to someone just inside the Luna's front entrance. In his favor, Meers was surrounded by a growing crowd as more and more people were pulled in as they passed by on the street. Meers slid through the crowd until he emerged on the Luna's side of the group.

"What did you say happened?" some local from the

Port Arms asked. "This one here said he heard something."

Meers deflected the questions with a simple, "It all happened so fast. I think someone headed that way, though." Saying that, Meers pointed in the opposite direction from the alley where he'd dropped his rifle.

Right on cue, most of the heads turned to look where Meers had pointed them. They gobbled up the misdirection just like the clueless guppies they were. When Meers looked back on it, he would surely allow himself a grin. For the moment, his face was all business as he stepped away from the crowd and stepped onto the boardwalk leading to the Luna's front door.

Reaching out to push the door open, Meers used his free hand to tap the little holster tucked beneath his jacket on his hip. The four-shot .22 was right where it was supposed to be. The pistol was so small that most people didn't even see it if they happened to look directly where it was stashed. It was so small that many people hadn't even felt it when its barrel was pressed against the back of their head. Even so, most folks wouldn't take too much comfort from having a hidden .22 when approaching a man like Clint Adams.

Adam Meers, on the other hand, got all the comfort he needed just by knowing the little gun was still there. If the Gunsmith stepped out of line, all four of those .22 caliber bullets would find their way into his skull. Meers knew from personal experience that that would be enough to kill any man.

Even a legend.

TEN

When Clint came downstairs, he had no choice but to head straight for the group congregating in the lobby. It wasn't a very large crowd, but they were all anxious and becoming more worked up by the second. The skinny old man who'd given Clint his key upon check-in spotted the new arrival and walked straight over to him.

"Mr. Adams, are you all right?" he asked.

Clint nodded and tried to look around the desk clerk. "Yeah, I'm fine."

But the old man didn't seem to be satisfied with that response and held Clint at arm's length like a tailor sizing up his fit. Either that, or possibly an undertaker.

"We heard the shots coming from outside," the old man said in a rush. "I even heard the body drop and, well, plenty of us figured it must have been you."

Clint was only surprised by that for a moment. Now that he'd heard it, all the strange looks that were being tossed his way seemed to make a whole lot more sense. Some of the others' faces seemed downright shocked just to see him on his feet and moving about.

"I'm fine," Clint assured the old man.

Although the clerk seemed relieved for a moment as

well, he soon took on a worried expression. Wincing
slightly, he asked, "Then may I ask who it is that you . . .
uhh . . ."

The clerk didn't have to finish the question for Clint
to know what he meant to say. The old man's nervous,
wide eyes centered upon the Colt at Clint's side told more
than enough for Clint to figure out the rest.

"I'm not shot," Clint said one more time for clarifica-
tion. "And I didn't shoot anyone." Pulling the old man a
little closer, Clint asked, "Do you recognize everyone in
here?"

The clerk took a quick look around and nodded. "Some
of the guests went outside, but yeah, I recognize most
everyone in the lobby."

Just then, Clint glanced toward the front door as it was
pulled open by a somewhat timid-looking man wearing a
plain dark suit. The other man hopped inside as though
he'd been pushed by the people milling around outside
the door and gave both Clint and the desk clerk a wavering smile.

"You didn't see my brother come through here, did
you Gus?" the man asked.

Up until then, Clint had forgotten the old man's name
altogether. Simply hearing it was enough for the clerk to
don his reflexive helpful smile.

"Brother? Can't say as I did," Gus replied.

"Mind if I check if he's all right?"

The clerk winced for a moment, but nodded anyway.
"Go on, since it's your brother and all. Just be quick about
it."

Tipping his hat, the plain-looking fellow headed for the
stairs and climbed them to the second floor. He was very
quick about it indeed.

Although Clint had heard the exchange, he was looking
for someone unfamiliar to the locals. Assassins had their
tricks, but living long enough in a community to be so

familiar with every last member of it wasn't one of them. Besides that, he'd spotted someone through the door as it had swung open that matched the description given by the young woman he'd caught in the upstairs hall.

Clint bolted through the door and looked around. At that moment, he was able to study the face of everyone out there since every one of the group turned to look at him the moment he'd charged outside. For the most part, they all looked as could be expected. Surprised, mostly, but also anxious to see more of the action promised by the shots they'd heard.

In just the short amount of time that had passed, the story had been retold so many times that the single rifle shot had multiplied into a shoot-out blazing from one building to another. The truth of the matter was considerably less exotic, but that didn't matter much to the dead Englishman with his pants still hanging around his ankles.

Hopping down from the boardwalk, Clint jogged over to the face that had caught his attention. The first thing he noticed was the way the other man pulled back with a look of true fear on his face.

"It's all right," Clint said to the entire crowd. "I'm not going to hurt anyone. I just want to find out what happened here."

As he spoke, Clint was focused mainly on watching that man to see how he would react and what it looked like he was going to do. Every second that passed so close to the Englishman's death was vital. An assassin wouldn't let grass grow under his feet before checking on his kill and getting the hell away from the hotel.

Unfortunately, the man that Clint had come out to see didn't seem to be in any particular hurry to do anything but throw in his description of what he'd thought he'd witnessed. Just like everyone else in the crowd, the man had his colorful story to tell and fought to tell it while still being heard over all the others. He didn't make a move to divert Clint's attention and, more importantly, was very close friends with several of the locals.

In fact, he turned out to be the desk clerk's nephew.

The instant Clint realized this, something dawned on him that made the bottom of his stomach drop. In the middle of yet another inaccurate retelling of the night's events, he spun on his heels and ran back into the hotel. He was breathing heavily as he charged straight up to where Gus was leaning against his desk.

"That man that went upstairs," Clint said. "Has he come back down yet?"

Judging by the look on the old man's face, Gus appeared to have already forgotten about the man Clint was talking about.

Fighting the urge to grab Gus by the shoulders and give him a shake to rattle the memory loose, Clint said, "The one checking on his brother."

"Oh! No, not yet."

Clint's stomach dropped even farther as he bolted up the stairs. On his way up to the second floor, he pictured the plain-looking man in his mind. What stuck out was, the little round spectacles he wore. They were the kind that were more common on men Gus's age.

They were also the kind that just might glint in the darkness if they were worn in a dark room just behind a window.

ELEVEN

Clint made it to the third step from the top of the staircase before stopping and ducking his head. Some folks might have called it foresight once the shot rang out from the other end of the hall and the bullet dug into the wood near where Clint would have been if he hadn't stopped. From Clint's perspective, however, it was just the voice of experience and common sense.

After all, he'd dealt with plenty of murderous snakes in his time.

The shot hadn't sounded like a large caliber, but any gun could cause a deadly case of lead poisoning. Moving quickly and in strong steps, Clint straightened up and took the last steps in two bounds. He pushed himself flat against the wall as soon as he reached the top and prepared himself for the shooter to show himself.

It was quiet in the hallway. It was quiet enough for even that small caliber shot to echo through the corridor like the grumble of distant thunder. Clint waited for a moment, but wasn't about to let anything grow beneath his feet, either. Keeping his hand over his Colt and every one of his senses on the alert, he stepped away from the wall and started walking toward the door to the English-man's room.

He made it there without so much as a whisper from anyplace else in the hall. Doing his best to watch what he was doing as well as the hall itself, Clint pushed open the door with his foot and glanced quickly inside. The dead man was still there. The window was still broken. The wind still blew the smell of blood through the room and into the hall.

Just as Clint looked down the hall, he heard the sudden rustle of feet scraping along the floorboards in another room just a little farther down the row. He leapt back until his back pressed against the opposite side of the hall, drawing the Colt in a flicker of movement the instant he heard Valerie's voice raised in a terrified scream.

"No!" she shouted from the room where Clint had told her to hide. "Get away from me!"

Knowing that he could just as well be running into an ambush, Clint held the Colt in front of him and rushed toward the room at the farthest end of the hall. He saw right away that Valerie's door was ajar and there was someone standing peeking out through the crack.

The next thing Clint saw was the glint of light off metal as a small gun was brought up and aimed in his direction.

Clint reacted out of sheer reflex, turning his wrist to adjust his aim before squeezing off a shot. The Colt's roar filled the hallway as smoke and fire erupted from the barrel. A chunk of the door blew apart from the whole in an explosion of charred splinters, leaving a blackened hole as well as a chipped jamb.

The figure that had been looking through the opening was no longer there. The sounds of more footsteps came from the room. They were light, quick, and headed deeper into the room.

Crouching down low, Clint reached out with his free

hand to push open the door as he charged inside. The damaged door flew inward and smacked against the wall, rattling on its hinges as Clint came through like a bull leading a stampede.

Inside the room, Valerie huddled against the wall near the bed with both arms wrapped around her head. She was fighting back another scream and the effort caused her to squirm and push herself tighter against the wall.

"It's all right," Clint said as he walked inside. Having seen her huddled there, Clint moved his eyes around the room in search of the shooter. "Where'd he go?"

After taking a quick peek to make sure who she was talking to, Valerie snapped an arm up and pointed toward the far end of the room. "That way."

There was an open window and a closed wardrobe in the part of the room where she was pointing. Clint walked up to the window, but kept most of his attention focused on that wardrobe. He would look outside once he got closer to the window, but there was no sense in discounting anything else inside that room. Such a mistake could be fatal if there was any chance that the shooter might still be there.

More experience gained after dealing with more than his fair share of snakes.

When he got to the window, Clint kept the Colt pointed at the wardrobe as he took a quick glance outside. The street below had some gawkers milling around, but not much else. The fact that those gawkers were milling, however, told Clint that an armed killer definitely had not just dropped down to the street and run off.

That left only one choice.

As if reading Clint's mind, the man inside the wardrobe kicked the door open and threw something out. The coat flew at Clint like a bat that had been scared from its perch and was deflected by a single wave of his arm. That motion bought enough time for the man to fly out next and slam all of his weight against Clint's torso.

Rather than take a shot without having a target in sight, Clint swung the Colt in a short, powerful arc which hit solidly against the other man as he tried to head for the door. When Clint got a look at the fleeing shooter, he found that the gunman wasn't fleeing just yet. Instead, he'd stopped and was aiming a small pistol from the hip.

The gunshots went off in quick succession.

In the middle of the other man's barrage, Clint had taken a shot of his own. The Colt's distinctive voice easily overpowered the smaller pistol, but at such close range, every piece of lead was just as deadly.

Another one of Clint's reflexes was common among any gunfighter who wanted to live through more than a few close calls. It was turning their bodies so that they stood sideways when facing their opponent rather than stand with their shoulders squared. That gave the other man a narrower target and gave Clint a long gouge across his back instead of a round in the stomach.

He wasn't sure how much damage his own bullet had done, except that it hadn't been a killing shot. That was no surprise since he didn't want to kill the gunman just yet. There were questions that needed to be answered.

Unfortunately, there wasn't anyone around to answer them.

TWELVE

Even as he went through the motions of looking for the gunman, Clint really didn't expect to find him. He poked his nose into every room down the hall as well as every other place the other man could have fled to, but he found nothing. For the time being, Clint was glad to have chased the killer away from Valerie, since she'd been the last person in harm's way. When he returned to her room, Clint was nearly knocked off his feet by the brunette's excited charge.

"Oh my God, Clint, is it safe?" she asked as her arms wrapped around him and she pressed herself against his chest. Her next question was difficult to hear simply because her face was buried against his shoulder. "Is he gone?"

"Yeah, he's gone."

"Are you sure?" Suddenly, her head snapped up and Valerie's brown eyes locked onto Clint's. They were wide, watery orbs. "Did you . . . kill him?"

Clint found himself running his fingers through her hair as a way to calm his own nerves as well as hers. He could feel Valerie's heart beating like a trapped sparrow inside her chest and her breathing was a constant brushing against his skin. "I didn't kill him, but you don't have to worry about him. Not for tonight, anyway."

"Not for tonight? Is that supposed to make me feel better? Where is he?"

"He's gone, Valerie. My guess is that he did what he wanted to do and is on his way out of here."

"And why aren't you going after him?"

Smiling, Clint held her face in his hands and said, "Because I'm here trying to make you feel better."

For a moment, Valerie simply stared back at him as though she didn't hear what he'd said. Then the words sank in and she melted into his arms. All the tension in her body and all the fear that had been building up flowed out of her and exhausted tears began streaming down her cheeks.

"I was so scared," she said. "I thought he was going to kill me for sure."

Clint didn't just agree that her life was in danger, he was pretty much sure of it. Of course, telling her that wouldn't have done anyone any good, so he patted her back and rubbed her shoulders until she was as calm as she was bound to get anytime soon. After she'd taken a deep breath, Valerie pulled away from him and nodded once.

"I'm all right now," she said. "Thanks for looking out for me, Clint."

"Speaking of looking out, did you see any other suspicious types coming from that hotel or the crowd in the street?"

She shook her head. Just thinking about that instead of what had just happened was enough to calm her down a little more and that was the entire purpose of the question.

"I didn't see anyone else, but the man that you chased out of here asked me the same thing."

Clint's interest perked right back up again. "Really? What did he ask you?"

"He asked what I saw or what I heard. I was too scared to tell him much, but I tried to make like I didn't know a thing. He didn't buy that for a moment and that's when he said he would have to kill me just to be sure. You know what struck me as odd?"

Clint didn't even know where to start on that one. Rather than say anything, he simply shrugged and shook his head.

"He said that he was sorry," Valerie told him with genuine disbelief in her voice. "He actually said he was sorry for having to kill me. Can you believe that?"

"It doesn't do anyone any good to try and figure out what goes on in a mind like that. I'm just glad you came out all right."

"Thanks to you." With that, Valerie practically jumped into Clint's arms and hugged him tightly. Her grip was a bit lower this time, however, and pressed down on the bloody gouge that had been ripped into his back by one of the gunman's bullets.

Although Clint tried to keep quiet, he couldn't keep down the sharp intake of breath and the pained grunt that rumbled all the way up from the bottom of his lungs. His face must have reflected the pain he was feeling as well because Valerie pulled back quickly and held him at arm's length.

"What's the matter Clint? You're white as a ghost!"

That was when she saw the blood on her arm and she immediately began to apologize while fretting with the wound she'd just stumbled over.

"Don't worry about that," Clint rasped. "I'll get it looked at in a bit. There's something I need to do first and I'm afraid you need to come with me."

THIRTEEN

"Whatever it is, it'll have to wait until you see a doctor."

"No, you need to come with me now. I need you to tell me about someone you might know from The One-Eyed Jack. Also, I don't want you out of my sight while I tend to another matter."

Without another word of explanation, Clint took hold of Valerie's hand and led her to the room where the dead Englishman was still lying. Along the way, he described Addy to her and asked about any unsavory business she might have been doing that went beyond what she normally got paid for.

"I know Addy," Valerie said, covering her eyes while Clint took a closer look at the body. "She'd do pretty much anything so long as there was enough money in it. Setting someone up to be killed like this is worse than I would have thought for her, but I'm not too surprised."

Nodding while listening to her, Clint looked over the body to see if anything jumped out at him as peculiar.

Valerie peeked from between two fingers and asked, "What are you doing?"

"Considering everything I've seen and heard as well as everything you've told me, this sounds like a professional killing. That man was an assassin, plain and simple. He did his job quickly and cleanly. He had an escape route planned out and he even figured a way to come back after any witnesses."

Hearing that last part made Valerie shudder. "If you want to go after him, maybe you should leave me and go," she offered. "A man like that can't be allowed to just walk around free."

Clint shook his head and met her eyes with a serious expression. "The only ones in danger right now are the witnesses and that's you and me. I also needed to get a look at this body to satisfy a hunch I had about this being professional or personal."

"Hunch? What do you mean?"

"A professional would need to report back to whoever hired him to kill this man. That employer would probably want proof that the job's done, especially if this man is as important as he seems."

Valerie swallowed hard and forced herself to ask, "What kind of proof?"

"The kind that the man they were after would probably only part with if he was dead. The kind that was distinctive and that could only come from him. This kind . . ." Clint replied as he lifted the dead man's arm by the wrist.

Martin Smythe's hand probably had never seen a day's hard labor. There were no calluses, no scars, not even any rough skin. There was, however, a finger missing. Judging by the amount of blood leaking from the stump and on the floor where the hand had been lying, it had to have been cut off recently.

"Oh my lord," Valerie groaned.

Clint set the hand down and stood up. "It's the ring finger that's missing," he said. "That's the proof the killer wanted when he came back here. Taking out the witnesses was his other goal."

"So you're going to find him, right?"

Clint didn't answer that right away. Instead, he took Valerie by the hand and led her out of the room so neither of them had to look at the corpse that was lying on the floor. The suite had a biting chill that seemed to come from something else besides the broken window. It was the kind of chill that hung around graveyards and made men believe in spirits.

No matter how many times he'd felt that distinctive chill of death, Clint never got used to it. In fact, there was a part of him that hoped he never did.

Stepping out into the hall, Clint noticed that Gus was standing far up on the staircase so he could peek out at what was going on in the upper hallway. Clint could hear commotion coming from downstairs as locals pulled together enough courage to get closer to where the action had taken place.

Without letting go of Valerie's hand, Clint walked the length of the hall. First off, he headed for the end opposite the stairway. Sure enough, there was a large window there which was still open. Clint peeked out carefully and saw that the window opened onto a large wooden overhang less than a few feet down from the bottom of the sill. From there, it looked like there was an alley or back lot of some kind.

"This is where he got out," Clint said, thinking out loud.

"Then go after him. I can handle myself from here on."

"This killer's a professional. He was out of my reach the moment he was out of my sight for more than a few seconds. He's either holed up in his safe house or riding out of town by now."

Valerie started to say something, but was cut off when Clint turned around sharply and took off toward the staircase. Gus was at the top of the case at that point, wringing his hands nervously.

"That man that came up here to check on his brother,"

Clint said. "Did you know him from somewhere?"

The desk clerk shrugged and shook his head. "I'm pretty sure I've seen him around lately, but can't say as I can put a name to the face."

Inside, Clint cursed himself for assuming too much when he'd thought that the clerk was familiar with the man in the spectacles. At least his mistake hadn't cost anyone else their life. Well, not yet anyway.

"The law's here," Gus said. "They want to talk to you two."

Clint's mind was already racing five steps ahead of where he was standing. Nodding quickly while still focusing on the plans he was building, he let go of Valerie's hand and said, "Good. You go with Gus here, Valerie. Tell them everything you saw as well as everything I told you. Can you trust the law in this town?"

Valerie seemed more than a little put off by that question. "Yeah," she responded. "The sheriff's my cousin."

"All right then. Keep close to someone you can trust and you should be all right."

"What about you, Clint? You're hurt."

"It'll keep. It's just a scratch. There's bigger fish to fry right now."

"You're going after him. . . . But I thought you said he had too much of a head start and that he did what he wanted anyway."

"I know what I said," Clint answered grimly. "But that doesn't mean he should get away with it."

FOURTEEN

Before he left the hotel, Clint checked the register at the front desk. It didn't take much to track down the Englishman's room number to find a full name. Even if he didn't know where the man had been staying, Clint would have been able to pick out the large, flourishing script which stood out like a sore thumb compared to the chicken scratches of the other signatures.

Not only did he get the name of Martin Smythe, but he also saw another name scribbled beneath it in a choppier, more sticklike script. The second name was Addy Rainer. Clint figured that was the name of the young woman he'd caught running from the room after emptying the Englishman's pockets. Sometimes hotels frequented by certain working girls made a note of their comings and goings just in case the women tried to pull any of their hustles on the wrong people.

Clint hadn't been expecting to find that other name, but it was surely a welcome bonus. He wasn't about to turn his nose up at any bit of luck that came his way. Even though the sheriff and his deputies were easy enough to spot in the crowd, Clint quickly stepped away

56

from the front desk before any of the lawmen spotted him and decided to ask Clint some questions.

Clint stepped out of the Luna Hotel and walked through the milling crowd like a knife cutting through butter. In the short amount of time that had passed since the actual shots had gone off, the crowd had more than tripled in size. Plenty members of that crowd recognized Clint, but they were more interested in watching where he was going than alerting the law as to the Gunsmith's whereabouts.

Walking amid the locals until he got to the side of the Luna Hotel, Clint went into the dark alley below the window at the end of the second-floor hallway. He kept his eyes locked on that window as he stepped out from the building and did some quick figuring as to how easy a jump it was—whether the shooter was making a getaway or tossing something down.

That latter notion caused Clint's eyes to travel along a somewhat different course. If something was getting tossed out, it would probably land against one wall of the neighboring building. On the other hand, if someone wanted to drop down from the window, they wouldn't have had any problem running along the overhang and making it to the street below.

The street was a little too well-traveled for there to be tracks that would stand out from all the others. Except, he figured, for the tracks made when the killer first landed after dropping down from the overhang onto the street.

Sure enough, when Clint looked down he didn't have much trouble at all finding one set of deep footprints that were in the right spot if someone was dropping down from above. Out of curiosity, he walked across the street and searched the area where something might land if it was tossed from the upstairs hallway of the Port Arms Hotel.

That general area happened to be occupied as well and

Clint stepped over to where a bundle lay in the dirty shadows against a wall. The bundle was long as a man's arm and appeared to be a blanket wrapped around something. Clint didn't have to see more than the little bit of steel poking out from one end of the bundle to know what was inside.

When he reached down and unrolled the bundle, Clint found that his eyes hadn't deceived him and that there was a rifle wrapped in the blanket. Some experts may have been able to tell for sure that the rifle was the one used to kill Martin Smythe, but Clint's gut told him all he needed to know.

The man in the spectacles had shot the Englishman, dumped the weapon and come over to the Luna to finish off the few people who'd spotted him as well as get the proof that would satisfy his employer. Although he hadn't tied up every loose end, the main task had been completed and he'd made a getaway out the Luna's window.

Clint nodded to himself as he reconstructed the events in his mind. Now that he'd gone through those motions, Clint was confident that he could accurately make predictions as to what was next on the assassin's schedule.

The kill was confirmed, so he would probably let things cool down for a bit.

The witnesses were still alive, so he might try to take one or both of them some time later when their guards were down or they seemed like easy pickings. Since the assassin appeared to be more interested in killing Valerie, Clint figured she would still be a target so long as the killer thought she posed a threat.

If time was more of the essence, the assassin might just be on his way out of town or lying low. It was possible that Clint's return fire had wounded him, so he may be licking his wounds somewhere as well.

All of these were short-term possibilities, but Clint didn't need to think too hard about the long-term ones.

The assassin needed to report back to whoever had hired him and let him know the job was done and things were well in hand.

This was one of those times that Clint was actually grateful for all the dealings he'd had with scum like hired killers and the like. He could learn how the lowliest weasel thought after tracking them long enough.

Clint could hear the sounds of approaching footsteps and voices that weren't going through any extraordinary lengths to keep quiet. Obviously, not everyone was as used to thinking like a killer as Clint was. Either the approaching men knew the assassin was long gone, or they didn't care enough to watch their step in a place the killer might be hiding. Since Clint had the rifle in his possession and was alone in both alleys, he doubted very much that someone knew too much more than he did.

As soon as the three men stomped into the alley, Clint knew he was right.

"Hey!" one of the three men shouted while fumbling for something at his hip. "Is that him? Is that the one that shot that fella?"

The other two squinted into the shadows and began to nervously step back. "Could be," another of them whispered.

Clint held out his arms, propping the bundled rifle over one shoulder. "My name's Clint Adams. I was a guest at the Luna Hotel. Where's the law in this town?"

"The sheriff is on his way."

Clint didn't know exactly which of the three men had answered him and at the moment, he really didn't much care. "Tell the sheriff I'll be getting in touch with him, all right?"

Two of the other three nodded. The remaining one was too busy trying not to look like he was making a slow retreat.

Moving slowly, Clint walked up to the trio and gave

them a wary smile. "Been a hell of a night, hasn't it?" he asked with an amiable shrug.

"Sure has," the taller of the three men replied.

All of them seemed to be more at ease when they saw Clint meant well and wasn't about to try to hurt them. They returned his smile and offered up a few bits of neighborly advice about keeping in the open until that killer was found. Once they'd said their piece, they let Clint walk one way as they went another.

Although they seemed to mean well, the three men didn't take more than Clint's word that he wasn't the killer. That just proved that the real assassin could probably have gotten past them just as easily. Clint shook his head and carried the rifle down the street toward another hotel he'd spotted near The One-Eyed Jack.

Hopefully the sheriff was better prepared to deal with this assassin. Unfortunately, Clint wasn't about to hang his hat on that one. If the killer was going to be tracked, the hunt would have to start there and then. And if the killer was going to be caught, it would require someone who knew what they were doing.

Since Clint had nothing else on his plate at the moment, he figured he might as well take the job.

FIFTEEN

Monroe's wasn't the biggest or smallest place in Port
Saunders. It wasn't the most expensive hotel or the least.
Like most others in town, it wasn't too far from The One-
Eyed Jack or the other saloons and it had a room available
that met Clint's heightened criteria.

Normally, he was satisfied with just about any place
so long as the door had a latch and the bed didn't break
under his back. This time, however, he didn't want a window looking into his room, and he wanted to be sure he
could hear what was going on in the hallway outside his
door.

The room at Monroe's was in the middle of the hall
with only a small window that opened onto the brick wall
of the building next door. Its bed was decent and the walls
were thin enough for Clint to hear every foot that landed
on the floorboards anywhere near his door. It didn't make
for the soundest night's sleep, but it was good for a man
who just might have an assassin on his tail.

Plus, it was cheap.

Since he wasn't sure how closely the assassin might
be following him, Clint made sure his door was locked
and his ears were open for any sound that could mean

someone was headed his way. For all he knew, the killer might not even be after him at all, but it never hurt to look over your shoulder a bit more than what was needed.

He looked through the room quickly. Mainly, he wanted to get the layout firmly embedded in his mind so that he could move efficiently in the dark if he needed to. Also, he was looking for a good place to stash the rifle. Just because the killer hadn't gone back for it yet didn't mean he was done with it for good.

Some men were downright religious when it came to their weapons. Even though Clint's modified Colt was no longer the cutting edge of technology, it was still a part of him just as much as one of his own hands. Seeing as how the assassin was more of a practical thinker, odds were that he saw the rifle as a tool that had served its purpose and had already forgotten about it after discarding it in the alley.

Either way, it belonged to Clint now and he aimed to get some answers from it. That would have to wait, however. Before settling into the room for the night, he needed to get back with the one loose end that might still have some of the assassin's interest.

Valerie was with her cousin the sheriff, which was probably the safest place for her at the moment. As more time went by, Clint was feeling more and more uncomfortable without having her in his sight. If something happened to her after he'd allowed her to leave, Clint knew it would be his fault. Some men might have called that irrational, but it wouldn't make Clint feel any better if he had to look down at Valerie lying dead somewhere.

The room wasn't much for hiding places. All he had to work with was a dresser that was too short to contain the rifle no matter how Clint could fit it inside and a table that was just big enough to hold a washbasin balanced on top of a folded towel.

That left Clint with one alternative, so he took out the

pocketknife he'd recently taken to carrying and stuck the blade into the side of the mattress. With a few sharp pulls, he opened a rip in the mattress that was big enough for him to insert the rifle, yet thin enough to be covered by the sheets which draped over the side. He made a note in the back of his mind to leave enough extra money to cover the mattress when he checked out and headed for the door.

It was somewhat strange how quickly a man's death could be absorbed and forgotten by the world around him. When Clint stepped out onto the street once again, folks passed by chatting and laughing as though nothing had happened. He heard a few wild stories and rumors about the shooting as he walked to the sheriff's office, but most of the talk was as though Smythe had died years ago.

The fact of the matter was that the Englishman was just another unlucky stranger who'd gone down in a fiery spectacle. The death was good fodder for saloon tales, but not very significant beyond that. Not very significant, of course, except to whoever had hired the assassin to take his life.

Clint couldn't stop thinking about what Addy Rainer had said about the Englishman being someone important in the government. If that was the case, then Clint knew there would be plenty more consequences than just some bloody stories tossed around in a saloon. Depending on just who Martin Smythe was, the repercussions could be downright serious.

Well, Clint's ace in the hole was that he'd done some work for his own government over the years. Every so often, friends of his in the Secret Service called on him to lend a hand to one of their agents or even act on their behalf. This time, he would be the one contacting them.

SIXTEEN

Adam Meers walked quickly, but managed to keep from running as he made his way from the Luna Hotel all the way to the small cottage that had been provided for him during his stay. The cottage wasn't much more than a furnished shack, but it was out of the way and had everything he needed during his job.

Whenever he'd passed someone, he'd returned whatever expression they gave him whether it be a cordial smile, a concerned frown or an excited stream of questions. No matter what, Meers had simply reflected the appropriate response without thinking about what he was saying or doing.

He didn't need to think. After all, most folks were only interested in what they wanted to see anyway. This was fortunate since Meers's thoughts were focused on his left leg which was a throbbing mass of fiery pain that sent shards of agony up through his spine with every step.

The speed of his steps and the dark color of his clothes brought little attention to the bloody wound on his leg. Considering that he'd gotten into a close-quarters gun battle with Clint Adams himself, Meers was pleased that he could walk away from it at all.

In fact, he was pleased that he was still drawing breath.

Throughout his years of work, Meers had studied up on the so-called dangerous men of the world. He separated fact from fiction more as a hobby since he rarely came into contact with such infamous and colorful figures.

Clint Adams was among that rare breed of men who lived up to their reputation and then some. Because of that, Meers knew that he'd only been shot in the knee because Adams had wanted to put him off his feet and not down for good.

Very unprofessional.

Letting out a labored sigh as he entered the small, shoddy cabin, Meers shut the door and dropped a thick board into the brackets on either side of the frame. The curtains were already drawn over the windows and within a few minutes, there was a small fire crackling beneath the blackened stone mantel.

Meers hobbled around the cabin, gathering up what he needed since he knew he wouldn't be up to standing again once he was off his feet. Every step he took ground edges of jagged, shattered bone against one another. The bullet had punched all the way through his leg, but it had done a hell of a job before leaving his body. Meers could feel the bones in his leg were close to snapping apart completely and it was his guess that the kneecap had been damaged as well. He figured out that second part by the near-blinding pain that stabbed from that spot every time he even thought about moving.

After collecting some rags, a needle and thread, bandages and a bottle of expensive Scotch, Meers made his way back to the chair beside the fire and lowered himself into it. Actually, he lowered himself halfway before the pain overtook him and he let himself fall the rest of the way. The chair creaked beneath him, but supported his weight.

Even letting out a sigh of relief sent a jolt of pain up

from his knee, so Meers grabbed the Scotch and poured
a healthy portion down his throat. The alcohol burned,
but in a good way as it drained down through his system
and started a little fire in his belly. Another swallow was
enough to take some of the edge off the pain, making his
movements a little easier to bear.

As soon as he felt the Scotch kick in, Meers took off
his boot and ripped the leg of his pants all the way up
past his bloodied knee. He could have taken off his pants,
but he wasn't crazy about the idea of getting up and going
through that particular process. With what he was getting
paid, Meers knew that buying a new suit was the last thing
he should worry about.

Surprisingly enough, the wound didn't look as bad as
it felt. Then again, for it to look that bad, his kneecap
would have had to be hanging by a thread from a bloody
cavern of a hole. All of that pain burned within him,
coursing through his entire body as though his blood had
been spiked with shards of broken glass.

Most people would have been paralyzed by that kind
of agony. Surely, even Clint Adams himself thought that
his bullet would have put Meers down for some time. But
Adam Meers hadn't gotten where he was by being as
weak as the normal man. He'd trained himself to either
ignore pain or fight through it so he could move on to the
next place he had to be.

It was either that, or be used for one job and thrown
away like most other assassins. The department that Meers
worked for went through most of their killers the way
Meers went through his weapons. They were put to use
once and left behind so that another one could take its
place. That made it harder for anyone to track down who
was behind the jobs, which was exactly the way Meers's
superiors wanted it.

But Meers was one of those few who was a career
assassin. Part of that was his ability to survive. That sur-

vival instinct was what allowed him to walk on a shattered kneecap. It also allowed him to sit by a fire, take hold of that kneecap with both hands and move it around until it was setting the proper way within his leg.

As he manipulated the shattered disk inside of him, Meers clenched his teeth so strongly that he would have bitten through his tongue if it had gotten caught in the wrong spot. The sound of cartilage grinding against bone filled his ears from the inside, crunching like wagon wheels against packed snow. Finally, he got the kneecap in its proper position and let out a loud breath as it fit into place.

The pain was still a raging inferno inside of him, but it had lessened somewhat. Every part of him wanted to let out the pressure that was building up like steam inside an engine. His legs wanted to kick against the floor. His fists wanted to beat against the chair and his voice wanted to let an agonized scream tear through the cabin.

But Meers kept every one of those instincts in check with one simple thought: if he gave in now, his career and life would be over.

The moment he lost his control, Meers was just another expendable asset who'd failed when he was needed the most. It had taken years for him to get where he was and it would take even longer for a replacement to get in that same place.

His job was important and his orders had been very specific.

There was no turning back. Not now, not ever.

Besides, he'd been in worse pain than this since he'd been given this assignment.

Focusing on all of that instead of what his hands were doing, Meers felt the pain melt away into a numbness. Of course, that numbness was helped along by the Scotch which he kept pouring down his throat. The only thing that mattered was that he was weathering the storm and getting his job done.

Right then, his job was to stitch up his wound using the needle and thread and then wrap bandages around his knee to hold it together and in place. Compared to manipulating his kneecap, sewing his flesh together was a relief. The needle hurt less every time it punctured his skin and by the time he tied the final knot, the pinched-together flaps were completely numb.

Compared to sewing the stitches, wrapping the bandages around his knee was another relief. The white material was wrapped tightly around his knee until it was both a dressing and support. When he tied that off, his entire leg was devoid of all sensation.

A couple more pulls from the bottle of Scotch and the rest of Meers's body lost its feeling as well. He didn't allow himself to get drunk. Fighting to keep his sobriety by focusing on the pain every now and then, Meers fell into a cautious sleep.

The fire burned itself out in less than an hour, leaving the assassin in total darkness.

SEVENTEEN

As Clint made his way through Port Saunders, it came to him that the town was arranged as though the planners had just tossed the buildings into the air and let them land where they may. The only place that had any order was the gambling district and that order stopped as soon as it became a bother to the saloon owners and card players.

Stores were scattered here and there on different sides of different streets. Houses were built wherever there was space for them. Stables and craftsmen's shops were spaced irregularly throughout the town and the sheriff's office was nowhere close to where it was needed. In fact, as long as the lawmen were in that office, folks could pretty much do whatever they wanted without worrying about being spotted or even heard.

Now that he thought about it, Clint decided that perhaps Port Saunders was arranged very well. Of course, that was only if he assumed that the town had been set up by gamblers and criminals.

Clint was laughing at that thought as he walked into the sheriff's office. His laughter was cut short the moment he saw that Valerie was alone inside the small, cramped room.

"Where is everyone?" Clint asked.

Valerie was on her feet and rushing to wrap her arms around Clint the moment he'd come through the door. She still gave him a big hug and kissed him once on the cheek. She was careful not to squeeze around the gouge in his back.

"My cousin's at the Luna, but he left some deputies here to look out for me."

As if hearing that statement, a pair of men with dim, hooded eyes sauntered in from the next room as though they were just coming in to sit down after a big meal. They looked at Clint with a curious expression, but didn't do much to satisfy that curiosity.

Clint's eyes narrowed as he looked at those two men. The only thing that set them apart from any other pair of lazy brothers was the badges pinned to their shirts. The longer they stared back at him without even saying anything, the madder Clint got.

"You're Clint Adams?" one of the deputies asked.

Clint nodded. "That would be me."

"I'm Darryl. And this," he said, pointing to the deputy beside him, "is Larry. We heard of you."

"Great. I'm taking Valerie with me."

Neither of the two deputies said anything, but Darryl nodded once.

Clint had plenty he wanted to say to the lawmen, but not with Valerie nearby. He was glad that she seemed calm, and he didn't want to do anything right then to upset her once again. Since he wanted to keep her in his sight for a while, Clint wasn't about to send her outside, either. That left him with only one choice: suck it up and leave.

"Where's the telegraph office?" Clint asked as he opened the front door to go outside.

Larry pointed toward the window as if that would be any kind of help. "Down the street a ways and on the left."

"I can show you," Valerie offered before taking the lead and dragging Clint out of the office. Once she was outside and the door was shut, she let out an exasperated breath. "If you didn't come for me soon, I might have broken those two's necks."

"Maybe I should let you back in there and give you a few minutes," Clint said half-jokingly. "You'd probably be doing the town a favor."

"My cousin was forced to hire them two to keep his job. It's a long story, but let's just say there's a good reason why they stayed at the office and the real lawmen went out to find that killer."

Clint fought back the urge to speak his mind about the fact that Valerie's cousin knowingly left her in the care of two chowderheads like Darryl and Larry when a professional assassin might be nearby. As much as he wanted to blow off some steam, he still didn't see the use in upsetting Valerie. So instead, he felt lucky that she was still unharmed and took her quickly to Monroe's.

The hotel was in sight when Valerie moved in a little closer to him and asked a question in a wavering voice. "Do you think he's still after me, Clint?"

"Could be. But if anything else was going to happen tonight, I think we would have already known about it. I meant to put a bullet in his knee to keep him from running, and I'm damn sure I hit him. He may just be somewhere tending to his wound or he could be out of town."

Valerie pulled in a quick breath and placed a gentle hand upon the bloody streak on Clint's back. "Did you see a doctor about this?"

"Not yet. I can send for one at the hotel."

"Better yet, I'll send for him. That way, I know you'll get that wound looked at before it gets any worse. I could use something to keep me busy anyway."

"That sounds fair."

He had to admit that it felt good to have someone fuss-

ing over him the way Valerie did. Her gentle touch felt
soothing on Clint's skin and her concerned words made
the night's events seem to weigh a little less on his mind.
Also, it couldn't hurt to have someone take care of him
since the deep gouge in his back was starting to cause
Clint more pain as the night wore on.

In the space of another hour, Clint was settled in his
room with a doctor examining the wound on his back.
The bullet had dug in deep, but not deep enough to graze
any bones. The wound was too wide for stitches, so the
doctor washed the wound out, bandaged it up and went
back to the poker game where Valerie had found him.

Even with the rifle stuck into the mattress like a steel
bar that ran under his shoulders, Clint felt better lying on
the bed, his shirt and boots strewn across the floor. The
room felt enclosed and safe and all the noises Clint heard
made him feel better simply because he could hear so
much of what was going on around him.

After turning the lantern down to its lowest flame, Valerie walked slowly toward the bed, peeling off her dress
as she went. She let all of her clothing drop to the floor,
curling next to Clint in a warm, naked bundle.

"Mind if I thank you for helping me tonight?" she
asked.

Clint laughed and stretched as he felt her hand wander
over his chest. "That bullet would have had to do a hell
of a lot more than scratch my back for me to say no to
that."

EIGHTEEN

Clint woke up a few hours before sunrise and found his way to the Port Saunders telegraph office. Due to the early hour, he didn't have to wait at all to get his message over the wire and on its way to the capital. He got a reply from Washington in no time at all, which wasn't much of a surprise since the line was monitored for important matters sent in by Secret Service field agents.

Normally, Clint would avoid using that contact if at all possible, but this seemed like a big enough matter to risk getting into a bit of trouble if he was wrong. Judging by the response he got back, Clint was nowhere near being wrong.

The ticker rattled off its code like a set of chattering teeth. That sound mixed with the scratch of the telegraph operator's pencil as the ticks were translated into letters and words. Once the ticking stopped, the operator looked down at what he'd written and handed it over.

"That'll be twenty-five cents," the operator said.

Clint flipped the coin onto the table and dropped a silver dollar right next to it. "Here's a little something extra," he said to the wide-eyed man wearing the visor.

"I'd appreciate it if you didn't let anyone know about my visit here or what any of the messages said."

Since both Clint's message and his response had been in sketchy language anyway, the operator really didn't know too much about what was in either message. He seemed more than happy to agree to Clint's terms and snatched up the dollar.

"Also," Clint added, "there's more in it for you if you let me know about anyone who asks about this or sends any other odd messages."

"It's . . . uhh . . . really against policy for me to tell you anything like that, Mr. Adams."

"All right then. I'll keep that in mind when I figure out how much more if I do hear anything else from you. You'll be especially happy if you happen to take a message from a man about my height with brown hair and spectacles."

That vague promise for more money was enough to seal the deal and the operator gave Clint a knowing wink. "Gotcha."

Clint gave the operator a quick wave and left the little office. Once outside, he unfolded the response and read it under the dim, purple light of approaching dawn. Already, the air was hot and sticky but what Clint saw written on the paper made his skin feel touched by a cold, steely hand.

The telegram read as follows:

ALREADY HEARD BUT THANKS FOR NOTICING **STOP**
COMPANY MARSDEN IS ON THE WAY AND SHOULD
ARRIVE SOON **STOP**
APPRECIATE WHATEVER FAVORS YOU COULD GIVE
STOP

Clint nodded, folded up the paper and stuck it in his shirt pocket. While there wasn't much as far as words on paper, the message told him quite a lot. The Englishman must have been someone important indeed if word had traveled that quickly all the way to Washington. Either that or they already had someone watching Port Saunders or some other nearby city.

Even though they already knew about what had happened and were taking steps on their own, it seemed that whoever was at the other end of that telegram knew Clint by name. That would explain why they asked for Clint's help so quickly. That didn't surprise Clint too much at all since the times he'd helped the Secret Service had turned out pretty well and federal agents weren't the type to forget who they could trust.

What did surprise him was that they were already sending someone to contact him. Marsden was the man's name and he was supposed to be there soon. The way Clint looked at it, the fellow had best show up soon because he surely didn't intend to wait around long.

Since Clint knew that the assassin wouldn't just be standing around at a saloon or kicking his feet up at a card table, it would have been an exercise in futility to go hunting for him just yet. Besides that, he needed to find out some more about the killer before seeking him out. Blindly hunting a murderer was a great way to stumble into the wrong end of a gun barrel.

Clint headed back to Monroe's and went straight up to his room. Valerie was waiting there for him, fussing with her clothing in front of the room's little oval-shaped mirror.

Spinning around to look at the door as he came in, she looked surprised at first and then smiled warmly at him. "Where'd you go off to?" she asked.

"Just went for a walk."

"I thought you might go to see my cousin."

"The sheriff?" Clint did his best to keep the sarcasm out of his voice. "No. I think I'll just stay out of his way and let him see what he comes up with on his own."

"I honestly don't know what he'll find. He's a good man and all, but I don't think he knows where to start with all of this. It's not like this kind of thing happens all the time. Usually most shootings are drunken fights or robberies or the like."

"There might not be much else to find anyway," Clint added. "Whoever this was knew what he was doing."

Valerie shuddered when she thought about the close call from the night before. "I've been thinking about it all so much. I just can't get it out of my head."

Clint had wanted to give her some time to calm down before starting in on the questions again, but didn't see any harm since she'd brought it up. "Have you thought of anything else? Like that man who came into your room. Have you seen him before?"

After a few moments of thinking, she shrugged. "The more I think back on it, the more it seems like a bad dream. I think I did see him at The One-Eyed Jack, though."

"What about the Englishman?"

Hearing that, her eyes widened a bit and she started nodding vigorously. "I know I've seen him before."

"Are you sure it was him?"

"Oh, yes. I heard some of the other girls talking about him. You know, the ones that make their living on their backs." Valerie added that last part like an insult that she wished she could have been delivered in person. "I never said I was a saint, but at least I can hold my chin up at the end of the day. Most folks don't see the difference in what I do."

Laughing, Clint shook his head and said, "I've played cards with you and I've seen the way you hustle at that table. Believe me, I know that's one hell of a skill you've got."

"Well, I wasn't good enough to get anything past you.

That's how I wound up buying you dinner, remember?"

"Of course I do."

"Those other girls say I'd make more money doing what they do." Her expression softened a bit as she said, "Some of them are my friends and just want the best for me. I know that sounds strange, but they're worried I might get killed by a sore loser someday.

"Anyhow, one of those other kind of girls was bragging about how they'd hooked a rich English fella who was spreading his cash all over The One-Eyed Jack. I'd lost a good amount to him earlier before this other girl started luring him away from the game. She made sure I heard about it because we don't get along and she thought it was funny she'd be getting my money off of him when it was all said and done."

"She sounds like a charmer," Clint sneered.

"She is. Right up until she steals whatever she can find in your pockets after you fall asleep."

"So did the Englishman tell you anything while you were playing cards?"

"Sure. There's always talk back and forth. He was quiet at first, but then he opened up once someone started talking about the war."

"The War Between the States?"

She nodded. "He kept shaking his head when Albert Wailing started talking about it. Al's an old rebel from way back but he's harmless enough. Mostly just a windbag, nowadays. Anyway, Martin talked about how nobody really knew what the war was about or what happened. He even said something about how the war's still going on. You ask me, I think he was just trying to rattle Al, because it sure as hell worked. That windbag couldn't think about much of anything once his feathers were ruffled."

Clint didn't have too hard a time believing that she could have been right. Distraction was as vital to poker as bluffing. It wasn't anything that could be found in any rule book, but neither was reading facial expressions or spotting tells. Any player worth their salt knew better than to be rattled by any of the talk around the table and it was something that many players didn't even try unless surrounded by novices.

But Clint wasn't as concerned with the gambling ruse as he was with what Smythe had said. Something in his gut told him that the talk about the war might have been coming from some kind of experience on the Englishman's part. It could have fit in with a background in the government or it might explain why Washington was keeping their eyes on him.

If Smythe was some important figure in the war, he might have advanced in the political ranks to still be a worthy target. Also, some degree of past influence might explain why he wasn't considered a top priority and only worth some modest degree of watching by the Secret Service.

"I wish I had more to tell you," Valerie said. "But that's about all I remember."

"Well, you keep thinking about it while I see what I can get from another source." Instead of leaving the room, Clint walked up to the bed and peeled back the sheets. The rifle was right where he'd left it.

NINETEEN

Valerie watched as Clint reached into the mattress through the slit he'd cut and fished around inside the stuffing. Just as she was going to ask what he was doing, she saw him pull his arm out and drag the long bundle from where it had been hiding just below the surface.

After Clint set the bundle on the bed and unwrapped the rifle, he pulled up a chair and sat down. His saddlebags had been draped over that same chair and he reached behind him to feel around inside of them without having to look as he rummaged through the familiar contents.

"Good lord," Valerie said in disbelief. "And I just thought the bed here was uncomfortable."

"It is," Clint said as he removed a folded leather pouch that was worn and discolored after decades of use. "Besides, you're not the one who spent the night with the hammer digging into your spine."

Curious as to what Clint was doing, Valerie walked around the bed so she could sit on it without disturbing the rifle. She sat cross-legged with her arms wrapped around her knees. "What is that?" she asked.

"It's either the killer's rifle or a Christmas present nobody found."

"What about that?" she asked, pointing to the leather pouch that Clint had taken from his saddlebag.

The pouch was slightly smaller than a cigar box. The leather was so worn that it conformed perfectly around its contents and had whitened lines running along the corners where the grain of the leather had been lost to age and use. It was rectangular in shape and tied up with a thick leather thong that looked about to snap at any second.

When Clint removed the thong, he set the pouch down and unrolled it until it was lying open next to the rifle. The pouch was actually slit on all sides but one, allowing Clint to open one half to reveal a set of tools that ranged in size from thin picks and screwdrivers to hefty pliers and a few that Valerie had never even seen before.

"These," Clint explained, "are my gunsmithing tools. Well, some of them anyway. Just the ones I might need when I'm not making a weapon from scratch."

"You can make a gun?" Valerie asked, clearly impressed by the prospect.

"Sure. That's the one story going around about me that's actually true."

She grabbed hold of her knees a little tighter and scooted closer to Clint's setup on top of the bed. The look on her face was similar to a little girl who'd just come to the best part of her bedtime story. "So what are you going to do to that rifle?"

The only time Clint really looked carefully at his tools was at the beginning to make sure they were all there. Having used them countless times before to clean and repair all kinds of weapons, he could have gone through all the proper motions in the dark if necessary. Selecting a tool from the open pouch while his eyes moved over the rifle, he picked up the gun and laid it on its other side, exposing the screws he needed to loosen.

"I'm going to take this rifle apart," he explained, "so I can get a look at the inside."

"Why? Is there something special about it?"

"Could be. Mostly, what I'm looking for is distinguishing marks. Sometimes hunters or assassins will make modifications to their guns so they'll work better."

"Really?"

Nodding as he sped through the process of disassembling the rifle, Clint kept his eyes open for any little thing that might be noteworthy. Talking to Valerie was more of a way to keep his thoughts organized and the brunette occupied while he worked.

"I've made some special modifications to my Colt. What someone does to their weapons can tell you a lot about that person. It could tell you how experienced they are or it may point you in another direction altogether."

Valerie folded her hands beneath her chin and watched him intently. Despite the fact that she didn't know exactly what he was doing, seeing Clint work with such speed and precision was impressive nonetheless. His hands flew over the blackened steel like each one had a mind of its own. He used the tools as though they were vital parts of him or extensions of his own fingers.

In no time at all, the rifle just seemed to fall apart under his efforts. Whenever a piece was separated from the whole, Clint carefully set it aside less than an inch from where it had started. By the time he let himself pause for a moment, the rifle looked like a diagram from a textbook. Each piece was by itself, yet all were close enough together for Valerie to see where they belonged.

The end result was as if the mechanism had simply been pulled in every direction until there was nothing left to pull. Clint looked down at it as he set his tools back in place within the pouch and then rubbed his hands together.

"Where to start?" he asked himself out loud.

Valerie let out a short breath and shook her head. "I knew there was more to a gun than just pulling a trigger, but . . . damn! Whoever thought to make something like this?"

"Someone who wound up very famous and very rich. Now, let's see what this piece of work can tell me."

Even though the disassembled rifle looked like a confusing mess to Valerie, Clint knew exactly what he was looking at. In fact, he hadn't even taken every assembly apart since that wasn't absolutely necessary for him to see what he needed to see.

It felt great for Clint to have his hands covered in gun oil again. His first love had always been building guns and making them work better after tearing them apart piece by piece. Compared to the art of smithing, firing the guns was just an afterthought. It was kind of like asking an artist to compare the acts of painting their pictures and hanging them on the wall.

Looking at the gun lying in all its separate pieces, Clint could hear the rifle's voice just as well as if he was firing it. He could tell how well the rounds would fit into the chamber and how easy the lever moved when loading another round to be fired.

But that wasn't all, he knew. There was plenty more the rifle had to say.

TWENTY

Clint picked up the pieces one at a time. He examined some longer than others before putting them back down in the exact spot where they had started. To him, the things he learned from his examination came as though it was plain for all to see. From Valerie's point of view, however, he might as well have been sifting his fingers through a heap of scrap metal.

"This rifle was pretty new," Clint said while looking closely at the hammer and firing pin. "Well, it's technically been around for about four or five years if I'm not mistaken, but it's only been fired a few times." Taking a longer look at the chamber where bullets were loaded before being fired, he added, "My guess is maybe only once or twice before last night."

Valerie nodded so as not to look completely stupid. She didn't get that impression from any way that Clint was acting, but she just felt like that since she had no clue what she was looking at. Apart from the fact that she'd seen the rifle completely assembled, she might not have guessed what any of the separated pieces truly were.

Clint was hardly paying her any mind. A couple times, he had to make sure she didn't knock something off the bed with an arm or leg, but he was mostly involved with the rifle. He picked up the barrel, rolled it in his hands to feel the weight and then looked straight down through the middle of the steel tube.

Nodding, he said, "It's military."

"You mean like from the army?"

"That's exactly what I mean. It might possibly have been sold to a civilian, but I doubt it. You see these modifications here and here?" he asked, pointing to a spot where the barrel connected to the firing mechanism and then to the inside of the barrel itself.

Nodding as though she knew exactly what he meant, Valerie managed to keep a straight face. Although she thought about asking him for more details, she figured they wouldn't help her much anyway.

Clint filled her in a bit more without being asked. "Those are mainly put onto army weapons so they'll better accept certain kinds of ammunition. Just a second."

Running his finger along the barrel, Clint came to a spot near the base that was rougher than the rest. He checked the firing mechanism and the stock as well and found similar spots that stood out as rougher. Each time he found one of those spots, he smirked and nodded slowly.

"These areas here," he said, pointing to the three spots, "are where there should be markings for the gun itself."

Scooting closer to him, Valerie looked where Clint was pointing. While she didn't know all the technical aspects of guns, she could understand what he was talking about just then. Not only that, but she found it interesting as well. "What kind of markings?" she asked.

"Either manufacturer markings or markings from the soldier who's issued the gun. There's also a marking to identify where it belongs in case it gets lost in a pile or something like that. Simple things really."

"And that gun doesn't have any of those markings?"

Clint shook his head.

Valerie's face brightened as she pointed out something that Clint hadn't mentioned yet. "Then maybe it's not from the army. It looks like plenty of rifles I've seen before."

"It's a Henry rifle," Clint said as if that fact should have been obvious. "The army uses plenty of them, but they can also be bought by anyone else all across the country."

"See?" Valerie said proudly. "There you go."

"But," Clint said, lifting a finger and pointing back to one of those rough patches on the stock, "if this was made for civilian use and sold by some gun store, the markings never would have been on the stock or side. They were there, but someone filed it off. Same thing with the manufacturer markings. They were there, but filed off."

"Why would someone do that?" Before Clint could answer, she snapped her fingers and said triumphantly, "So nobody would know where the gun came from. Is that right? Would anyone really be able to tell any of that by those markings?"

Clint smiled and said, "You win the prize. Actually, those markings don't tell a whole lot unless you know what to look for. Mostly, it's just like someone writing their name on their property or putting a tag on something so you know where it belongs. The odds are pretty slim anyone would be able to tell much if they found this gun and saw the markings intact.

"The point of the matter is that whoever used this gun didn't want to take the slightest chance of being tracked. There might have been slim odds with the markings, but with them scratched out, the odds are next to nothing. In fact, this gun might as well not exist any longer. I can't tell where it was made, who it was made for, or where it was shipped."

Letting out a frustrated sigh, Valerie said, "So this has all been for nothing?"

Clint shook his head. "I wouldn't go that far. First of all, the fact that those markings were removed tells me that this gun was prepared by someone who not only didn't want to be found, but who really knew what they were doing to prevent it. These details are too small for most killers to even worry about.

"Also, I know for a fact this gun was intended for use in the army or maybe even the U.S. Cavalry. It was kept somewhere for a while and only used this one time."

"I thought you said it was fired a few times before."

"Yeah, but that was probably just to set the sights and make sure it worked properly. Before that, it was probably waiting somewhere until it was needed. This looks like a five- or six-year-old model at least. No later than that, though."

After taking one more look at the rifle pieces, Valerie moved back and climbed down off the bed. "Well, since he dumped his gun, maybe that killer won't be heard from again."

Clint shook his head. "I'd really like to believe that, but I think there's more to it than that. This just proves that the assassin has some careful backers in the military and he's patient enough to wait for years to do whatever job he's been given."

"Then maybe we should just cut our losses before we get pulled into this thing any further."

Thinking about the telegram he'd sent to Washington, Clint felt a sinking feeling that started from the bottom of his boots. "It's too late for that. I'm in this up to my eyeballs."

TWENTY-ONE

Clint reassembled the Henry rifle without even needing to think about what he was doing. Apart from the things that weren't there, the firearm was so clean it might as well have still been in the glass case at a gun dealer's shop. He entertained thoughts of just dumping the damn thing in an alley and taking Valerie's advice, but his own words were still fresh in his mind.

It was too late for that.

Although it seemed more than a little ominous, Clint took the statement as plain and simple truth. There was already someone on the way from Washington and dodging that person would only make Clint look guilty as sin if anything else happened remotely connected to the assassin. Even worse was the fact that there was no doubt in Clint's mind that there would indeed be more happening in that regard.

As he placed the rifle back inside the mattress, Clint could feel tension filling up the room like a fog that came from both himself and Valerie. When he looked back at her, he found the brunette sitting on the other side of the bed with her back to him. Even by just looking at her back and shoulders, he could tell that she was about to break from everything that was weighing down on her.

Walking around the small room, Clint sat down beside her and let a couple silent moments pass before saying a word. Finally, he placed his hand on her knee and squeezed it comfortingly. "Probably some of the best advice I ever got was to not worry about anything until there's something to worry about."

Valerie let out a short laugh. "I'd say there's plenty to worry about."

"Well, we're not sure if the gunman is even still in town and we don't know if he's still after either of us. We can't sit in this room forever, that's for sure. All we know for certain is that we'll both starve to death if we don't get out of here soon. At least, I sure will."

This time, Valerie's laugh was genuine. "Typical man. The world could be falling down around your ears and you'll still ask what's for dinner."

"Aren't you hungry, too?"

"I guess."

"And wouldn't you like to get out of this room? I know I picked it out specifically, but it sure as hell wasn't for the comfort or view."

Valerie looked up to the tiny square window which in turn looked out onto a brick wall and laughed again. "Maybe I could pull myself away from this place for a little while."

That was all that needed to be said to get both of them straightened up enough to leave the room. Actually, Clint was already presentable, but Valerie insisted on fixing herself up a bit. She took some time at the water basin and used one of the towels provided by the hotel.

Dipping the towel into the water, she slowly ran its wet tip over the back of her neck, dabbing at the droplets that ran down her shoulders. Looking up at the ceiling, she peeled down the front of her slip and rubbed the wet towel over the top of her breasts. Before turning her back to Clint, she arched her back which pressed her erect nipples against the material restraining them.

Watching her was a particular treat for Clint. He found his eyes following every stray drop of water as it rushed over her skin before getting caught by the towel wrapped around her hand. Even after she'd put her back to him, he was captivated by the curve of her spine as her slip became wetter and wetter so it could cling to her flesh.

Just as the thin material started sticking to the upper curve of her buttocks, she looked over her shoulder and handed back the towel. "Could you dry my back for me?" she asked. "I'm getting awfully wet."

The suggestive comment was as plain as the fact that she was nowhere near being truly embarrassed to let Clint see her front. On the other hand, there was plenty to be said for the direct approach and Clint felt his body respond instantly to the sultry tone in her voice as well as the beautiful sight of her body displayed in front of him.

"Sure," he said, trying to keep some degree of detachment in his own voice. "Let me get that for you."

He took the towel and began gently rubbing her shoulders as well as the back of her neck. From there, he started dabbing along the area where her skin was covered by the back of her slip. All he had to do was nudge the material a few times before Valerie responded accordingly.

"Here," she said. "Let me get that for you."

With a shrug of her shoulders, the straps holding the slip over her breasts came down and the top of the garment peeled away even farther. Still standing behind her, Clint used the towel to slide the clothing all the way down her back until he could just see the curve where the small of her back gave way to her firm, rounded buttocks.

Clint still moved the towel over her body, working his way along her sides until his hand brushed against her stomach and then worked up toward the bottom of her breasts. Rather than say a word to him, Valerie arched her back and pressed her shoulders against his chest, sighing quietly as both of his hands enclosed her breasts.

Standing with the front of his body pressed upon her back, Clint felt his penis stiffening the more Valerie rubbed against him. She shifted her hips until her buttocks moved up and down against his cock, rubbing it until his erection was rigid and full.

"You're doing a good job," she purred while placing her hands around both of his wrists. Guiding his touch down over her stomach until his fingers were between her legs, she said, "But I'm still awfully wet. Can't you tell?"

He could tell all right and the moment his fingertips slid along the moist lips of her vagina, Clint's entire body ached for more. A hunger raged from deep inside of him, guiding his hands as he reached to hold her tightly against him while working to get out of the clothes which were restraining him.

The moment he unbuckled his belt and dropped his pants to the floor, Clint reached past Valerie and shoved the washbasin off the table. It landed with a loud shatter and broke into several pieces on impact. That noise caused Valerie to pull in a surprised, excited breath as her eyes went wide with anticipation.

She moaned with even more anticipation when she felt Clint's hand press against her shoulders, pushing her down until she took hold of the small table with both hands. Her fingers wrapped around the edge of the tabletop as she spread her legs apart a little more to allow Clint to get closer. Arching her back while lifting her head, Valerie closed her eyes and waited to feel what she'd been aching for this entire time.

Clint moved his hand down along her back and felt the hot, wet surface of her skin. Grabbing hold of one hip, he used his other hand to guide his cock between her thighs until he felt it slide into the warm, moist embrace of her pussy.

They both let out a moaning breath which was like a release of the tension that had suddenly built up between them. Clint slid all the way inside of her until his hips pushed against the soft flesh of her buttocks. Valerie allowed her head to drop down as she was filled up by his thick column of flesh.

It had happened so quickly that she could already feel her orgasm building from within as Clint took on a steady, pumping rhythm. He moved his hands over her back for a little while before resting both of them upon her hips so he could drive into her a little harder.

The table knocked against the wall and the room began to fill with their loud, excited breaths. For that moment, there was nothing else in the world that mattered. No assassins or dead bodies.

Just a man and a woman indulging their own desires. Everything else would just have to wait.

TWENTY-TWO

Meers spent the night unconscious in his chair with one eye trained on the cabin's single door. Although most people would have called it sleeping, that was too comfortable of a term to match Meers's reality. Sleeping was lying somewhat comfortably and relaxing until morning. What Meers had done was sit still just long enough for consciousness to leave him.

There was no comfort.

There was no relaxation.

It was the same way he'd lived through most every moment for the last decade of his life.

When he came to and felt enough energy in his body to move, Meers pulled himself to his feet and bit back the pained scream that raced up to the back of his throat. Agony pulsed from his kneecap as though he was being punished for his sins and he damn near made a noise to alleviate a bit of the pain.

But the only noise he made was a snakelike hiss as a controlled exhale squeezed out from between clenched teeth. The world wavered around him and the floor seemed to tilt beneath his boots. Rather than grab on to the chair for support, Meers focused all his attention on controlling the pain and taming it.

In the space of a few terrible seconds, he got himself together enough to move on. The first step was almost impossible to take. The next one was a little easier and the one after that was even easier. Although the pain was still an inferno that seared him from the inside out, he got a tighter grip upon it with every step.

Finally, he was able to walk with only a slight limp and the expression on his face could be made to seem somewhat normal. With those things under control, he gathered his things, packed them into a saddlebag and carried that bag with him through the front door.

It was early morning and already there was plenty of activity on the streets. The first people he came across lived nearby and nodded in a friendly way as though they'd known him for more than a few days. Meers returned the nod along with a little small talk, all the while making his way to a little building a few blocks away.

By the time he arrived at the telegraph office, Meers had all but put his pain completely out of mind. His thoughts had moved on to bigger and better things. Mainly, he was concerned with the exact wording of the message that he was about to send over the wire. If the wording wasn't exactly right, it would be discarded without a second thought. If he said the wrong things or not enough of the right ones, he might find someone very much like himself coming to end his life.

As assassin's work was as precise as it was dangerous. Only the careful ones made a living at it. Even the best of them died from it.

What kept Meers going was the fact that his work was so very important and he knew deep down that he was the most qualified man to do it. Besides all of that, he'd been wrapped up in the same job for so long that he no longer knew any other way. It wasn't that he didn't want to take any other options. For him, there simply were no other options.

The door to the telegraph office swung open and the scrawny old man in the black vest behind the little desk gave him a quick nod and a wave. "Good mornin'. Fine day out there, wouldn't you say?"

Meers returned the wave and smiled cheerfully. "A fine day indeed. Is it too early to send off a message?"

"A few minutes ago I would have said yes," the old man replied as he quickly hid a plate littered with the remains of some scrambled eggs and toast under the desk. "But I can't put off working all day right?"

"Sadly, no."

There was something about Meers that put the clerk at ease. The older man felt he was in good company and had an instinctive impulse to let his guard down around the friendly, well-dressed man. There was no good reason for him to feel that way, but it was understandable that he did. After all, Meers was a professional.

"I was just about to make some more coffee," the clerk said. "You care for some?"

"No, thanks. I just need to send off this message and be on my way. Thanks for the offer, though."

Meers fought back the urge to say something when the clerk took his time getting himself situated and settling in behind the desk. The old man moved like he was among friends and that neither of them were in any particular hurry to be anywhere or do anything. That was the drawback to getting past people's guard. Meers didn't necessarily like it, but he dealt with it the way he dealt with the rest of life's pains.

Rubbing his hands together when he was finally ready, the clerk said, "All right, then. Where's the message going?"

"Washington, D.C."

The clerk's eyebrows went up as he scribbled in the

correct line of his form. He smirked and shook his head as he got the more specific information on where the message was headed.

Watching the older man, Meers took note of his reactions. He began studying the clerk very carefully, although he gave away nothing by the way he was looking at him. He stood the same way and wore the same smile, but his thoughts and senses were working doubly hard to try and see if there was more to the clerk's peculiar response.

Meers wrote down his carefully plotted, albeit short, message and slid it over to the clerk so the words could be tapped into the wire. There was nothing for the older man to see in the message since each word meant something else entirely.

Even so, the older man seemed to spot something that brought another curious look to his face.

"What's the matter?" Meers asked good-naturedly. "Did I spell something wrong?"

"Oh, not at all. It's just that . . . well . . . have you ever felt like you've already done what you're doing?"

"Oh, yeah. All the time. Did someone else send a telegram to Washington today?"

The clerk started to speak, but caught himself. The look on his face was more than enough to tell Meers that something was wrong. It also answered the question he'd asked without the old man having to say another word.

Meers put on his best disarming smile and leaned onto the counter with one elbow. "You know, there was a time that I talked to a man for ten minutes and I swore I knew what he was going to say right before he said a word of it. It was really strange, but I swore that I'd already talked to the fellow and was just remembering it then."

The story was complete bullshit. All Meers had to do was mirror the clerk's response and what little the older man had given him while wrapping it up around a short anecdote. The rest was just speaking in a soothing voice and playing on the friendliness that had already been established. The rest worked just fine on its own.

"So maybe those kind of strange things just happen," Meers said after finishing up the little story. "You know what I mean?"

The clerk nodded, thought it over for a moment and said, "I really do know what you mean." He leaned on the counter just the way Meers had done and lowered his voice to a whisper. "Don't tell this to anyone else, but there was a fella in here right when I opened for the day."

Meers listened to the older man and nodded as though he was only slightly amused. Inside, every word he heard was etched into the stone of his infallible memory.

TWENTY-THREE

From the moment she put her clothes back on, Valerie couldn't wipe the smile off her face. Even through breakfast, she was in better spirits than she would have thought possible only a few hours before. Since there wasn't a whole lot of other options, she took Clint's advice and only concerned herself with things that she could control. At the moment, she felt she could enjoy her day and the company she was in.

Unfortunately, Clint wasn't so quick to take his own advice. He put on a somewhat convincing performance when Valerie was talking to him, but his mind was much too concerned with everything going on that he couldn't see. He just couldn't shake the feeling that Martin Smythe's assassination wasn't the last. Also, he was about to burst waiting for the arrival from Washington to find him.

At least he didn't have to wait long before one of those things was resolved.

Clint and Valerie were walking toward the telegraph office when something caught Clint's eye. If he wasn't looking for anything unusual around him, he might have missed it. As it was, the little peculiarity stuck out to him like a sore thumb.

As the crowd flowed around him, walking across the street and up and down the boardwalks, it appeared to be one thing moving like a body of water in various directions. Looking at the crowd as a whole, the movement seemed to be a constant, which made the few people standing still jump out from the rest.

Apart from those who were simply standing still for a moment or talking to one another in front of a shop, there was a man dressed in a pearl gray suit with a matching bowler who caught Clint's eye. He was clean-shaven and didn't appear to be past his late twenties. Intense eyes and a solid jawline gave him a naturally handsome appearance, but his stiff posture and severe expression kept most other folks moving right past him.

For Clint, the young man in the gray suit caught his attention instantaneously. When he stared across the street at the fellow, the younger man didn't look away. Instead, he nodded once and started walking straight toward him.

Apparently, the young man had caught someone else's attention as well.

"Well, well," Valerie said with a smile in her voice. "It looks like I might just have to split my time up among two handsome suitors."

"Maybe," Clint responded. "That is, of course, so long as you like government types."

"What do you mean?"

Clint didn't answer her question. Instead, he waited for the other man to get closer so he might answer the question on his own.

"Clint Adams?" the man in the gray suit asked.

"That would be me."

A smile cracked the other man's face, but only slightly. The smirk didn't quite suit him and even looked a bit uncomfortable the moment he put it on. "I'm Hugh Marsden with the United States Secret Service."

"Now that is what I call service," Clint said. "You got here awful quick."

"I received word from Washington not long ago and took the first train here." Seeing the disbelief still present on Clint's face, he added, "I was stationed in San Francisco."

"Ah. That makes a bit more sense."

"Is there somewhere we can talk?"

Clint looked over to Valerie with a victorious smirk that he wore without the slightest bit of discomfort. Looking back to Marsden, he said, "Sure. Why don't we head over to a favorite place of mine. Folks there give each other their privacy."

"Sounds fine." Marsden looked over to Valerie and his eyes reflexively looked her over quickly from top to bottom. He may have been serious in nature, but he was still a man.

Valerie waited for the other man to look into her eyes before she smiled and extended her hand. "Pleased to meet you. My name's Valerie."

Marsden took her hand and shook it once. "I'd like to talk more with you later. For now, though, would you mind if Mr. Adams and I talked alone?"

"I know everything he knows," she said. "You can talk in front of me."

"Sorry. That's just not possible."

They were less than a block away from The One-Eyed Jack. Clint stepped back into the conversation before she could fire back with a more colorful response. "We're almost at the place I was telling him about, Valerie. This will go a lot quicker if we just go along with our government man here." Leaning in closer to her ear, he added, "See if you can find Addy and ask her about the man that paid her to be with the Englishman."

Although Marsden didn't seem to appreciate being left out of that little exchange, he didn't make an effort to get closer to listen in on Clint's whispering. He did seem happy enough when Valerie nodded, turned on her heels and left them alone.

Looking up at the front of the gambling hall, Marsden shrugged and said, "I'm not sure how safe this place is, but if you insist."

Clint shrugged as well, doing his best to look indifferent to whatever complaints Marsden had. "I'm not too familiar with this town at all. It's either talk in there or wander the streets like vagrants."

Marsden was already walking toward the front door. By this time, Clint had gotten a good enough look at the other man to tell that Marsden was wearing a shoulder rig under his jacket and had another holdout pistol in a holster on his right boot. Regardless of who the other man worked for, Clint felt much more comfortable knowing who he was dealing with.

The moment they got inside the place, Clint and Marsden headed for the same empty table near the back of the room. As soon as they were out of earshot of most everyone else in the place, Marsden looked Clint in the eye and laid his cards on the table.

"I'm not accustomed to working with types like you, Mr. Adams, so let's keep this brief. I need to know everything you saw or heard regarding the matter of Martin Smythe and I need to hear it as quickly as possible."

Clint eased himself down into a chair and leaned back casually. "What's the hurry?"

"Frankly," Marsden said, taking the seat opposite of Clint's, "I don't expect you to live through this day."

TWENTY-FOUR

Clint let that last comment hang in the air for a moment without a reply. He waited because of the smiling redhead wearing the low-cut dress who was coming toward their table. The curvaceous waitress tried to flirt with the two men, but quickly saw that neither of them were all that receptive. Since there were plenty of other customers that were more than willing to tip for a look down the front of her dress, she took their drink orders and walked back to the bar.

"That's a hell of a thing to say to a man," Clint said. "I assume you've got something to back it up?"

"I do."

"Are you going to tell me or is it confidential?"

Marsden glanced over his shoulder and saw that the redhead was coming back with their drinks. He kept his mouth shut until both mugs were placed on the table and some cash was handed over.

All the while, Clint watched the Secret Service agent with careful eyes. He could tell the other man was fairly new to his job since he'd been around more experienced agents—specifically his old friend, Jim West—and could sniff out the difference between Marsden and someone more accomplished in field work. Also, there was an underlying nervousness to the agent, which Clint could detect from another area of experience.

Once again, his poker senses were serving him well. If Marsden was playing cards with him, Clint would have figured him for someone with a good mask, someone holding a mediocre hand at best. Since Marsden was working on something involving Clint's life, that nervousness had a tendency to be infectious.

"All right, Adams," Marsden finally said. "My orders are to hear what you have to say, so start talking."

"Who sent you here?" Clint asked.

"I told you. The United States Secret Ser—"

"Not that. I want the name of the man who contacted you."

"How is that important here?"

"Because I want to know who to rip into the next time your Service contacts me for help." Leaning forward so that he could glare even more intently into Marsden's face, Clint said, "I've done plenty of work and probably closed as many cases as you have, but without the kind of pay that allows me to buy your kind of fancy suits.

"I could've just put this business behind me, but I sensed it was kind of important, so I decided to do the right thing and wire Washington. If my help's not appreciated or if you really can't stand my type, just let me know and I'll be on my way. Otherwise, I'd appreciate it if you wiped that smug look off your face and pay me just a bit of damned respect."

Clint was exaggerating slightly about the amount of work he'd done for the Secret Service, but thought he was fairly accurate about everything else. The certainty in his voice combined with the unwavering intensity in his stare was enough to seal the deal.

Once again, Clint had years of bluffing to thank for seeing him through.

Where Marsden had been holding himself with blatant superiority before, he now shrank down a bit into his chair and fought to maintain his confident expression. The cracks in his facade showed, and he allowed his guard to drop a bit.

"Fair enough, Adams," he conceded. "It wouldn't be appropriate for me to mention any names, but you did come highly recommended by someone I trust. This whole matter is just a bit . . . unusual, to say the least."

Clint let his intensity cool off a bit and raised his glass. "Much appreciated. Now, how about we start again fresh?"

Marsden took a sip of the beer he'd ordered and was about to set his mug down when he stopped with it hovering half an inch over the table. He then lifted the mug back to his lips and drained almost half the brew before letting out a breath and setting the mug down solidly.

"I needed that," Marsden said in a voice that was drained of much of its former tension.

Clint couldn't help but laugh a bit at that. "I was just going to say the same thing."

"You might want to drink a bit more of that yourself, Mr. Adams, before I say what I came to tell you."

"Go on and spill it. I'd rather get on with this than wait anymore."

"Suit yourself. The man who killed Martin Smythe used to work for the United States government. He's part of a small group of assassin-sharpshooters that were used during the War Between the States to eliminate certain threats to national security. He is an exceptional killing machine, but that's not the worst of it."

"It isn't?" Clint asked. "What's worse than that?"

"We don't have control of him anymore. In fact, nobody does."

Clint nodded as he took that in. Then he tipped back the mug and downed every drop of his beer.

TWENTY-FIVE

Meers didn't make a big show of things. In fact, even his most important jobs all started out as a series of seemingly insignificant acts. This one was no different.

As soon as he got the telegraph clerk to tell him just enough to let him know that Clint Adams had also been talking to Washington, Meers shrugged off the talk as interesting gossip. It seemed that the clerk thought it wasn't much more than that either and only casually asked Meers to keep the talk to himself.

"Of course," Meers had said. After that, he tipped his hat, took his own folded response from Washington and left the office. After that barely memorable exit, Meers would never be seen in that office again.

He walked back to the cabin to check over it one more time, making sure that he'd cleaned it up properly. One change of clothes and a fresh set of bandages later, he left the cabin and set off for the stables.

One of the best parts of keeping track of someone as widely known as Clint Adams was that most everyone else did all the work for him. All Meers had to do was look like just another curious nobody who would be impressed to hear any story about the Gunsmith and people were more than willing to tell him one.

That went with saloon owners, card dealers and even people who worked in stables.

Meers only had to go to one other stable apart from the one where his own horse had been until he caught up with Adams's black Darley Arabian stallion. The horse was impressive and the stable owner even let him get a closer look for a small fee. Blocking out the stable worker's babble, Meers took in all he needed to see and then tipped his hat by way of thanks.

"I sure hope Mr. Adams doesn't get too upset knowing you let me look at his horse," Meers said with just the right amount of apprehension in his voice.

The stable worker shook his head and winked. "He doesn't have to know."

"Well, he won't hear anything from me. Thanks for your trouble."

With that, Meers left the stable and got onto his own horse. He drew little to no attention by taking his time and ambling out of town as though he was only out for a midday ride. The moment he got far enough away from Port Saunders, he touched his heels to his horse's sides and snapped the reins. Just to be sure he wasn't being followed, he rode for half a mile in the wrong direction before doubling back once he was on higher ground.

He spent almost an hour watching the trail he'd left behind before he was satisfied that there wasn't anyone else coming after him. If there was someone following him and he hadn't spotted them by now, Meers figured that he probably wouldn't spot them at all. Rather than waste time worrying about possibilities, Meers climbed back onto his horse and pointed its nose southeast toward his true destination.

As he rode, he thought about the loose ends that still needed to be tied up in Port Saunders. Leaving witnesses wasn't something he was used to doing, but he also wasn't used to getting targets snatched out from under his nose the way Adams had stolen away that brunette.

Unfortunately, there wasn't anything he could do about them just yet. There was a schedule that had to be kept, otherwise his remaining targets might just slip away as well. That brunette could be taken down at any time and a man like Clint Adams wouldn't be too hard to find. Losing a target, on the other hand, was completely unacceptable.

Once targets started getting away from him, Meers knew he might as well retire from the business before another killer was sent out to retire him for good. He was in for a couple days of hard riding before he got to where he needed to be. That would allow him to settle in and watch his next target for a day or two so he could pick out the time and place to make his move.

With that next target dead, he would have enough time to track down Adams, kill him and then come back for the woman. Despite the impressive reputation of the Gunsmith, Meers didn't think he would have much difficulty taking him down.

Every man let his guard down sometimes, which meant he could be killed.

Adams seemed like the sort who didn't stir up trouble, which meant he wouldn't have what it took to stop a professional assassin before it was too late.

Meers smiled and nodded to himself as he rode. Killing Adams would be one hell of a credit to his name. Perhaps he should find someone willing to pay him for it. He doubted there was any shortage of folks wanting to see Adams dead. They would pay even more if they could take credit for it.

In the end, Meers didn't care who got the credit just so long as the job got done. Either way, Clint Adams was as good as dead.

TWENTY-SIX

Clint wasn't normally the type of man who relied on alcohol as a way to deal with his problems. He'd seen too many sorry-looking souls draped over too many bars to allow himself to take much comfort from a bottle. Every so often, though, a beer or two did wonders to cancel out the taste when he had to swallow some bad news.

Even after two beers, the news Clint got from Hugh Marsden still tasted bitter in the back of his throat.

"So let me get this straight," Clint said. "You work for the same people that paid this Meers fellow and now you're telling me that even you can't call him off?"

Marsden nodded without any emotion on his face. "That's right."

"And who was Martin Smythe? Was he someone high on someone's shit list or just some poor Englishman who was in the wrong place at the wrong time?"

"Smythe was an important man, that's for sure. He was more important during the war, however."

"Important enough for his life to be in danger?"

Marsden nodded. "Exactly. He worked for the British government as a liaison between them and us. He handled a lot of supply issues and was pivotal in deciding who got what as far as weapons and financial support.

"There were plenty of deals going back and forth during the war, since both sides needed help wherever they could get it. The official deals were one thing, but the unofficial ones were something else entirely. Lots of times, a hell of a lot more changed hands under the table."

That sounded only too familiar to Clint. He'd gotten his fair share of offers to work for the law and even the government, but had passed on every last one of them. The political nonsense that Marsden was describing was exactly the reason why.

Pausing to let a passing couple move farther away from them, Marsden continued in a slightly quieter voice. "Smythe took money from both sides. Officially, he helped supply the federal army with guns and other military supplies. Unofficially, he made sure the rebs got enough to keep them going."

"The longer the war went on," Clint said, "the longer he could keep making his sales."

"Precisely. And he wasn't the only one. Everyone that was contacted for aid during the war brought profiteers along with them. It became known that both sides were being approached for the sake of making money. What's more, it soon appeared that the rebs were being sold guns earmarked for federal soldiers, which was the same as weapons and money being stolen right from the United States Treasury. At the time, President Lincoln figured all of this was an unavoidable evil. He called it a 'dirty part of an even dirtier business' and was more concerned with ending the war than chasing after thieves."

"That sounds like something he would have said." Even as the other man had said those words, Clint could imagine them being spoken by Lincoln's deep, somewhat gruff-sounding voice.

"He might have said it, but not everyone in the capital heard it. There were plenty of men in high positions who didn't like anyone stealing from them and just having to take it."

Clint immediately thought of at least half a dozen comments and jokes to make about that, but kept them to himself.

"These men," Marsden continued, "were in a position to watch these profiteers closely. Before too long, these profiteers started selling information as well as supplies to the Union troops."

Clint hardly had to hear another word. "And that's just what they were waiting for, wasn't it?" he said. "After all, if one side is being sold information, then the other side is probably getting its fair share as well."

"That was the conclusion that was drawn, yes."

"And with the possibility of information being leaked, that was all these other higher-ups needed to put a price on the heads of these profiteers. That way, they could take them out one way or another and say it was official business."

"The only problem with that was the president," Marsden said. "He found out about the proposed . . . um . . . solutions and put a stop to them personally. It was a messy business, which was complicated even further by the war itself and the unfortunate incident afterward."

Focusing his eyes on Marsden, Clint made his next statement as blunt as possible so he could watch how the other man would respond. "You mean when Lincoln was killed. That's the unfortunate incident you were talking about?"

Marsden didn't flinch at Clint's words or the tone in which they were spoken. The muscles in his jaw tensed slightly and some of his previous coldness returned. "Yes, Mr. Adams. That's what I was talking about."

Clint nodded slightly and leaned back in his chair. "Just making sure." And he *was* just making sure. Mainly, he wanted to be sure how Marsden felt about the loss of the president. His reaction there spoke volumes about the agent's character as well as where he might fit into this whole situation regarding Adam Meers.

From what Clint could read off the agent's face, Marsden was still sitting on the right side of the fence.

"There are several branches of the government that will never appear on any document, Mr. Adams. Many agents work in the dark and only answer to one or two men. Several of these operatives work without ever meeting their superiors face-to-face and whose existence would be denied by every office in Washington."

"You're talking about assassins, right?"

"Yes. Several of these agents were sent out to deal with the privateers discovered during the war. Most of them were recalled without a problem."

"And what about the rest?"

Marsden shifted uncomfortably in his seat and took a drink of his beer. "Most were taken care of."

Not wanting to get into how, exactly, those agents were taken care of, Clint said, "The war's been over for over twenty years. Are you telling me there's some killer out there who either doesn't know that or doesn't care?"

"Meers was put on standby until other more pressing matters were wrapped up."

Clint smiled more out of the irony of the situation rather than because he saw any humor in it. "I see. Would those other pressing matters be killing those assassins who were also on the government payroll?"

"I can't discuss that with you, Adams. You know this." Although those were the words coming from Marsden's mouth, his eyes told Clint that he'd been right on the money.

"All right," Clint said, letting his previous question drop. "So why would he go after Smythe now?"

"Actually, that's what I was hoping you'd find out."

"Excuse me?" Clint said. "Last time I checked, I wasn't one of your agents for hire."

"No, but you do a good job for us when you're needed. You were there when Smythe was killed and even got a look at the killer. That means you're in a perfect position to help us now."

"And why would I do that when I could just wash my hands of this whole thing?"

"Because you're not that type of man, Mr. Adams."

Clint had to admit that the agent was right about that. Still, he wasn't about to say that to Marsden.

TWENTY-SEVEN

"Why don't you just recall him yourself?" Clint asked. "If he's one of your men, surely you can get hold of him much easier than I could."

"We've tried contacting him several times. There was never a reply. In fact, we thought he'd been killed until targets from that old list of privateers started coming up dead."

"You mean there's been more than one?"

Marsden nodded. "Smythe was the fourth. Let's just say the first three weren't the kind of men that any respectable people would miss. Certain people in the Service noticed, but weren't sure the killings were related until Smythe became a target."

Leaning his head back so he could rub his eyes, Clint let his brain absorb all of what he'd just learned. Getting a personal visit from a man like Marsden was never a good thing. Being offered a job by an agency that has former employees disappear on a regular basis was even worse.

What made Clint's head ache just a bit more, however, was that he was still waiting for the really big punch to land.

"The problem is," Marsden went on to say, "that the remaining people on that list have gone on to more respectable positions since the war. A few of them have even risen in stature within the governments of other countries. If they continue to be killed, the repercussions could be catastrophic."

And there it was. The words felt just like a punch to Clint's stomach, even though he'd been preparing himself for them the entire time.

Marsden felt the weight of what he was saying as well. In fact, he even winced slightly when he put the topper onto the entire speech. "We may even be talking about another war."

"I don't suppose you'll tell me who else is on this list of yours?"

"The list is confidential information, Mr. Adams."

"Of course it is."

"But," Marsden added with a raised finger. "I can tell you one of those names."

"Just one? Why's that?"

"To give you someplace to start catching Adam Meers, of course."

And there was the follow-up punch.

"Your life is already in danger, Mr. Adams. So is that of the woman who you rescued last night."

Clint didn't even bother asking how much more Marsden knew since that information was more than likely confidential as well.

"He'll be coming after you both more than likely sooner rather than later," the agent said. "So you're already in this."

"I know that," Clint shot back. "I'm the one who contacted you, remember?"

"I certainly do. That's why I was informed you'd probably be open to seeing this through for us. You've gotten closer to Meers than any of us have since General Lee surrendered."

"And Meers probably knows all of the men you'd send after him on a first-name basis. Am I right?"

Reluctantly, Marsden nodded.

Clint took a moment to think everything over one more time. Even though he'd had a feeling that there was more to the Englishman's murder than what he could see right away, he didn't think there was the possibility of war hanging in the balance. He knew Marsden wasn't about to map everything out for him, but he could pretty much figure it out on his own.

Any man with serious connections to the political machine of any town had his fingers in a whole lot of pies. Those connections just got bigger once they were put on a national level. It only went up from there once the connections spanned more than one country.

People would sit up and take notice that Martin Smythe was dead. Important people. More than that, they weren't likely to be happy that he was assassinated. If the British government found out that their man had been killed by an American assassin, the shit would most definitely start to fly. Wars were started for lots of reasons and Clint knew that most of those reasons were based on money and power. There were some good reasons to go to war, but those were tossed in as icing on the cake. It all turned out the same.

War.

Violence.

Death.

"All right," Clint said. "Besides me and Valerie, who else does Meers want to put in the ground?"

TWENTY-EIGHT

It didn't look like Addy would be too hard to find.

Once Valerie had left Clint alone to deal with the well-dressed government man, she started searching for the young girl who was the last one to see the Englishman alive. She had no trouble believing that Addy might have had something to do with getting Smythe killed. After all, there were plenty of working girls who wouldn't mind something terrible happening to one of their clients.

The sad truth of the matter was that plenty of the men that slept with those girls deserved something bad to come their way. Valerie knew that only too well, which was why she'd started earning her money lying at a card table instead of lying on her back.

When she didn't spot Addy right away, Valerie made her way around the gambling hall, catching up with old friends. Many of the working girls in town still had their hearts in the right place and a few were actually more than willing to point her in the right direction.

"What are you lookin' for her for?" one of Valerie's old friends asked. Before she got an answer to the question she'd just asked, however, that same girl shook her head and said, "Never mind. Don't tell me. I probably don't want to know. Last I saw Addy, she was talking to one of those Elder brothers at the Black Tail Saloon."

Valerie motioned to the bartender and placed a few coins in front of him once he arrived. "These are for the next few rounds of whatever my friend here wants."

"Oh, you don't have to do that, Val," the other woman protested. "Just make sure Addy gets some of what's coming to her."

"The least I can do is buy you a drink or two. Lord knows this isn't the first favor you've done for me. And don't worry about that second part," Valerie added as she glanced over to where Clint and Marsden were sitting. "Something tells me Addy's got a full plate right now."

The other working girl ordered her drink and leaned in close to Valerie as soon as the bartender left to pour it. "Does this have something to do with that Englishman that was shot dead last night?"

"Actually—"

"No, wait! Never mind. I don't want to hear it." Smirking, she followed Valerie's gaze and spotted Clint right away. "That's Clint Adams isn't it?"

"You sure you want to know?"

"I know it is! Is it true what I heard about him?"

Rather than give her the long version, Valerie winked, nodded and said, "A lady never tells."

"And since when did you become a lady, you little thief? Either fill me in or I'll tell your Gunsmith over there how you get all that money you toss around at the card tables."

"Later. How about that?"

"It'll have to do, but don't you dare forget about me."

"I won't," Valerie insisted. "Not with the kind of blackmail you have on me."

With that, Valerie checked on Clint one more time before stepping away from the bar. She could tell that he and Marsden were wrapped up in their own conversation and probably would be for some time. That was just fine since that gave her some breathing room to do some tracking of her own.

Besides, she figured she wouldn't need any help in dealing with the likes of Addy Rainer. At least she'd never needed help before.

TWENTY-NINE

The Black Tail Saloon was one of those places that was never very busy, yet somehow managed to stay in business. It was never busy because most folks could tell just by looking at the run-down place that the shifty-eyed people drinking there were up to no good. And if there was one thing that outnumbered the amount of shadowy corners inside the Black Tail, it was the number of dangerous figures standing in them.

Valerie knew about the place only too well by reputation alone. In her earlier days of working on her own, she'd tried looking for paying customers there. It only took a few black eyes and even closer calls for her to learn why the other working girls steered clear of the place. As a gambler, she avoided it even more simply because players got themselves killed over much lesser things than simply cheating.

Just because she didn't like going in there, Valerie put on her best smile and walked through the batwing doors with her head held high. The swinging doors rattled behind her, both of them ready to fall off their hinges simply because of all the bodies that had been thrown through them over the years.

As soon as she entered, Valerie could feel the eyes taking her in with a hunger that sent a shiver down the middle of her spine. She knew only too well what it felt like to have men desire her. In fact, she'd used that to prosper in two separate occupations. But what she felt in the Black Tail was more than just lust. It was hunger.

It was the kind of hunger a coyote felt for a smaller animal who'd been dumb enough to leave its jugular exposed.

The man who approached her not only looked at Valerie the same way, but his smile reeked of that hunger and worse.

"Hey there, Val," the slimy-looking man said. "It's been a long time."

The man's name was Bret Elder. His hair might have been brown, but it looked a shade closer to black the way it was greased against his scalp. He had the build of a gorilla with huge arms and a barrel chest. His face looked a bit too small for his head and came complete with a pair of dark, squinty eyes.

Valerie maintained her confident smile and gave the man a nod. "Hello, Bret. Is Addy around?"

"She's over talking to Randal. Why don't you keep me company until they're through with their business."

Randal was Bret's brother. Although he was somewhat leaner than Bret, Randal still had the Elder features, which made him look every bit as shifty as the first Elder man who'd come to town.

Valerie dismissed Bret's proposition with a wave and walked over to a table farther into the saloon where she'd spotted Addy. "I need to see her right now. Besides, I'm sure that they can pick out a place to climb on each other just as soon as I leave."

Just when she thought she was going to get past Bret without any more fuss, Valerie felt a hand close roughly around her arm. Not only was she stopped from going any farther, but Valerie was also pulled back a few steps so roughly that she felt hot pain inside her shoulder. She kept from showing that she was hurt, but Bret could sense what he'd done no matter how brave Valerie tried to look.

"Let go of me," she said in a fierce tone of voice while spinning around to face him once again. Even though she tried to wrest her arm out of Bret's grasp, she simply wasn't strong enough to do it now that he wanted to keep hold of her.

The greasy man smiled at the attempt she made to get away from him. He pulled her in a little closer so he could prove his strength over her even more. "Don't worry yourself none, Val. I'll make sure you get to see Addy. Why don't you just relax and have a drink with me? It's been a long time."

"You already said that," Valerie shot back. "And if it was up to me, it would be even longer until I see you or your no good brother again. Now let go of me because I guarantee you won't like it if I have to ask you again."

When Bret pulled in a slow, deep breath, it sounded like the hiss of a massive snake. The excitement on his face was plain as day and it only grew the more Valerie tried to break away from him. "I like it when a girl talks like that. If you would've done more of that in your whorin' days, I might have called on you more."

Valerie's gut response to that was to reach for the derringer that was waiting in a pocket hidden within the folds of her skirt. It was easier to get to than the one strapped to her thigh and she'd practiced for a long time to perfect the motions necessary to draw and point the little gun. Her draw was quickened by the anger she felt inside of her, but it still wasn't enough to get more than a loose grip around the weapon's handle.

Without taking his eyes from Valerie's breasts, Bret snapped his other hand around Valerie's fingers. Now holding both her elbow and hand, it looked as though the unlikely couple was engaged in some kind of dance as she struggled to get away from him and he kept pressing closer.

Bret's grip tightened around her fingers until he could feel bones mashing against the handle of the derringer she'd tried to draw. "What were you gonna do with this?" he asked. "You gonna shoot me with that little gun when all I wanted was to stick it into you one more time?"

Listening to Bret's words and feeling him spit on her face as he said them was almost too much for her to bear. What infuriated her even more was that she couldn't seem to do a damn thing to stop him. Valerie kept trying to turn the pistol toward Bret even though she was clearly outmatched by the strength of his one hamlike fist.

"You can stick it into a hole in the wall for all I care," she said angrily.

Bret's lips curled into a humorless grin, revealing two rows of chipped, crooked teeth. "Nah. I think you'll do just fine."

He pulled her a little closer and thrust his hips forward until his crotch bumped against Valerie. She could feel his erection through his jeans and turned her head so he wouldn't see the fear and dread written all over her face.

At that moment, Valerie was fairly certain she wasn't going to leave that place alive.

THIRTY

In the other part of the room, Valerie could see faces turned toward her and Bret. They watched intently, but it was obvious not one of them was concerned for her safety so much as they were interested in what was going to happen next. She knew they would watch her being beaten, raped, or even killed the same way they'd watch a stage show.

Not one of them would lend a hand to help her get away from Bret Elder. After all, why would they want to end the show?

"Stop it," came a voice from the back of the saloon.

Valerie looked in that direction hopefully and was just in time to see someone stand up from where they'd been seated. The person standing up was Addy Rainer and the only reason Valerie hadn't recognized the other woman's voice was because she'd never heard Addy scream before.

With Addy's plea still echoing throughout the shadowy room, there came a dull thumping sound as Addy was knocked off her feet by a strong backhand. That sound was quickly followed by the thump of her backside hitting her chair and the scrape of wooden legs skidding a few inches over the floorboards.

The man who'd hit Addy had the same greasy features as Bret Elder and enough similarity in the eyes and mouth for him to obviously share blood with the bigger man. Randal Elder had a leaner build, but still carried some extra weight around his midsection. His narrow face gave him more of a ratlike appearance which was accentuated by his thin, wavering smile.

"Shut up," Randal snapped. "Let my brother finish his business so we can finish ours."

Addy wanted to say something, but flinched reflexively at the thought of being smacked down again. She started to slip out of her chair, but stopped when she received a stern look full of mean intentions from the man sitting beside her.

Once it was clear that he'd put Addy in check, Randal nodded to his brother and leaned back in his chair.

"Looks like it's just you an' me, bitch," Bret snarled victoriously. "You wanna do this out here for everyone to see or should we go in the back so we can have our privacy?"

Shifting her expression into something a little more friendly, Valerie fought to keep her mask from slipping and to keep the shakiness out of her voice. "If there's a bed around here, I might even start to enjoy it. And if we're alone, I can let my hair down a bit more."

Although he obviously wasn't sure of what to make of her sudden change of heart, Bret's face showed the slightest bit of hopefulness behind all the bluster. To Valerie, that glimpse might as well have been announced by a fanfare.

Her mind raced as she was turned toward the bar and pushed in the direction of a sturdy-looking door marked by a sign that read PRIVATE.

"Now that's more like it," Bret sneered as he tightened his fist around Valerie's hand. He kept squeezing until he could feel bones grinding against metal and joints scraping together.

As much as she wanted to hold on to the derringer, Valerie simply couldn't withstand the punishment she was being put through and had to relinquish her weapon. The instant her fingers loosened from the pistol, Bret's hand enveloped the gun and took it away.

"You're a smart lady," he said while dropping the pistol into his back pocket.

"Not really," she answered, struggling to keep up as he half led and half dragged her across the room. "I would just rather fuck a filthy pig like you instead of get raped by one."

In the face of that insult, Bret merely grinned wider and nodded. "Yeah. You are a smart lady."

As they got closer to the door behind the bar, the rest of the saloon started turning back to its own business. Seeing that the show was pretty much over, drinkers went back to their glasses, gamblers went back to their cards and partners went back to their negotiations.

"She a friend of yours?" Randal asked once he, too, lost interest in what his brother was doing.

Addy was shaken up by what she'd seen mainly because it hit too close to home for comfort. Shrugging defensively and forcing on a smile, she replied, "Not really."

"Good. Because I'd hate to think that you'd hire me to do what I'm going to do to a friend. Makes me wonder what the hell you'd do to an enemy."

"Killing her is one thing. I'm not paying you to have your brother torture her or . . . worse."

"Worse to you, maybe. Fun for him." Randal shifted so he could watch as Bret and Valerie still dragged their feet toward the door behind the bar. "Maybe fun for me, too."

It wasn't too often that Addy felt ashamed of herself. In her line of work, she'd set aside feelings like bashfulness and shame as a matter of course. That way, she was more free to take the extra steps that might have been considered harsh even by other working girls' standards. Still, there was an uncomfortable chill that worked its way through her system when she thought about what would happen the moment Valerie was taken through that door.

In another attempt to think about anything else, Addy shook her head as if she was shaking rain from her hair. "You shouldn't do this," she said suddenly. "This ain't what I was paying for. This ain't a part of our deal."

When Randal turned to look straight into her eyes, he had more of that animal look about him. "You didn't pay me yet, so we don't have a deal."

"Here, then," Addy said as she tossed a folded wad of cash onto the table. "Take your money. Kill her and the other one, but I don't want your brother to take her back into that room. Just because she's no friend of mine doesn't mean I want to sit here while that happens to her."

Randal took the money and ticked it into his pants pocket. "You can leave then."

"And you'll tell your brother to stop?"

"Nah."

"But that's not part of our deal!"

"Then he'll do it for nothin'. And when he's done, so will I."

THIRTY-ONE

They were behind the bar and almost to that door. Valerie hadn't been fighting as much as before, but she still dragged her feet and struggled whenever she could. She made a show of taking her time, justifying it by stumbling over chair legs, returning looks from drunks, or even flirting with Bret himself.

In her mind, she tried to imagine the door wasn't there. She tried to convince herself that none of it was happening. She even tried to take away the knowledge of what would happen the instant Bret was given the privacy he was after.

"I've got a room of my own you know," she said. "It's got a big comfy bed and I could even slip into something for you."

"Oh, so now you're anxious to put a smile on my face, huh? You think I'm stupid?"

"No. You'll have to pay me. You said you'd pay me before if I treated you right."

Bret smirked at her obvious attempts to keep him occupied. Even though he knew what she was doing, that didn't mean he didn't enjoy the attention she was giving him. On the contrary, it seemed as though he was actually starting to feel comfortable with her. At least his grip was beginning to loosen around her arms.

The front door of the saloon opened and a man walked inside. Valerie couldn't see who it was because Bret was a mountain of flesh in her line of sight. "Is that the sheriff?" she asked in a last-ditch attempt to divert Bret's attention.

The big man might not have had a head full of brains, but he knew better than to turn around at that one. Instead, he smiled, shook his head and continued pushing her toward the door.

Although she couldn't make out any details, Valerie saw the front door close and a minimum of activity happening near the entrance. There weren't even any words exchanged beyond the bartender's standard greeting. She felt her heart sink right down along with her hopes once even that little bit of commotion faded away completely.

Bret reached past her to open the door. Almost immediately, she was overcome by the stench of stale cigarette smoke, mold and rotting wood. She resisted the impulse to look behind her into the room itself, but was forced to glance back when her heel caught on a board that was higher than the rest on the floor.

Valerie started to fall, but was held up by Bret's hands. A far cry from saving her from the spill, Bret left her dangling from his fists and dragged her all the way into the room. Once inside, Valerie was surrounded by the dirty stench, which was now accompanied by the scuttle of little feet as rats scuttled back into hiding.

"You don't want to do this," Valerie said, her words spilling out of her in a desperate flow. "I can make you feel so much better if you give me a chance."

Bret let go of one arm just long enough to shift both her wrists into one of his hands. He used his free hand to reach between Valerie's legs and grope awkwardly under her skirts. The instant his fingers touched her smooth, naked flesh, he smiled like it was Christmas morning.

"You're gonna make me feel just fine," he snarled while pressing his erect penis against her thigh. "Don't you worry about that."

THIRTY-TWO

It was one of those horrible moments that Valerie had only experienced once or twice before. Most people would only know that kind of horror once, if ever in their lives. At that second, Valerie couldn't have been more envious of those more fortunate souls.

Just then, the door swung open, but Valerie was on her back with Bret looming directly over her and she couldn't see past his lustful smile. A familiar voice drifted into the small, dirty room.

"Hey," it said. "What do you think you're doing?"

For the briefest of seconds, Valerie had some hope that a savior had come. That hope lasted right up until she recognized the voice as Randal Elder's.

Bret recognized it even before she did and made no effort to take his eyes off of what he was doing. "You wanna watch," he said, "just don't get in the way."

Listening to every sound and absorbing every sight like she was in a nightmare, Valerie noticed something strange about Randal's voice. Mainly, it seemed to be coming from the other side of the saloon, which meant either something was wrong with her ears or Randal wasn't really close enough to open that door.

At that moment, she saw a shape move up from behind Bret's hulking body. It happened so quickly that all she could see was the shape descending on the bigger man half a second before a hand landed roughly upon Bret's shoulder.

Those fingers closed so tightly on Bret's shoulder that they seemed to disappear within the other man's shirt and skin. From Valerie's point of view, it seemed as though the other person's fingertips dug all the way into Bret's flesh, impaling him like four curved spikes.

Bret's face twisted slightly more out of surprise than pain, that expression growing even more as he was pulled back forcefully and tossed onto his side against the closest wall. "What the hell?" Bret growled as his eyes snapped around to see what was going on. "You ain't Randal!"

"Well, well," Clint said in a mocking tone of voice. "You might not be as dumb as you look."

The barrel-chested Elder brother pushed back with both feet until he was edging his shoulders up the wall. One hand reflexively grabbed for his gun while the other was still fumbling to keep up his pants which he'd already unfastened.

Clint practically flew across the room, covering the distance in two long strides. It looked as though he was about to take another step, but instead that leg swung straight forward and buried a boot deep into Bret's gut.

The air rushed out of Bret's lungs and his entire body went limp. Although he still managed to hold on to his gun, he didn't have the strength to lift it up and take aim. Clint was already reaching down to pluck the weapon from his hand. Unfortunately, Bret didn't have the good sense to know when he was beaten.

Clint gave the other man a second to do the right thing. It only took half a second to see that Bret was about to do anything but the right thing. The moment he saw Bret's fists balling up and his eyes turning into fiery coals, Clint snapped his hand out and across, smashing Bret's pistol right into the big man's jaw.

"Then again," Clint said as Bret teetered and then finally dropped over, "you may be a little dumber than I thought."

When Bret hit the floor, he stayed there and his eyes glazed over. Clint turned to check on Valerie, but found her already up and on her feet, charging toward him with her arms open wide.

She gave him a powerful hug and kissed him passionately on the lips before he could say another word. Then, just as suddenly, she leaned back and gave him a swat on the shoulder.

"What took you so long?" she asked breathlessly. "I stalled him for so long that I thought you weren't coming at all."

"You're lucky the bartender at The One-Eyed Jack knew where you were going or I wouldn't have found you at all. Thanks for letting me know you were leaving, by the way."

Valerie was too exhausted to say anything else. Instead, she headed for the door and stopped the instant she looked into the saloon's main room.

Striding past her, Clint froze as well before he was fully out of the back room. Just about every man in the saloon had his gun out and was pointing it at Clint and Valerie.

"That's him!" Randal Elder shouted. "A hundred dollars to whoever puts him down!"

THIRTY-THREE

When he'd walked into the Black Tail, Clint's first instinct was to take a quick look at all the faces he could see. As far as he could tell, the saloon wasn't much different from a thousand other holes he'd visited in countless other towns. The faces were dirty and the eyes were shifty. Every one of them wore their guns in plain view and were obviously itching for a reason to use them.

There was no doubt in his mind that any of those men would have killed blood relatives for half of what the man in the back was offering. And it was because of those conclusions he'd already drawn about the men in that bar that Clint was already prepared to act even before he'd stared down the barrels of all that drawn iron.

Clint's left arm shot straight out and he twisted his torso around until he felt his elbow make contact with Valerie's body. Using the palm of his hand, he shoved her back and down while continuing his turn until his shoulders were lined up to the rest of the saloon. From there, Clint dropped to one knee and drew his Colt in a motion that was so fast, it nearly escaped the naked eye.

He did all of this in the space of a heartbeat. Even so, it seemed to him like he didn't have nearly enough time before the front room of the saloon erupted into a series of explosions. With so many targets to choose from, Clint had no way to pick out which one should be his first. He did, however, manage to spot the man in the back who'd given the order to start firing.

Clint had no idea who that man was, but it was obvious he was intent on doing some major damage. For that reason alone, Clint pointed the Colt at Randal Elder and squeezed off a shot as hell broke loose all around him.

So many shots were fired at once that they seemed to blend into one clap of thunder which rolled through and filled the saloon. The smoke from all those barrels spewed forward and hung in the air to form a dark, gritty curtain between Clint and the rest of the men inside the place. Fortunately, Clint managed to take his shot just before that curtain fell and he caught a glimpse of Randal reeling back after the bullet drilled through him.

Although Clint's first instinct was to turn his face away from the thick layer of smoke, his instinct for survival was stronger and kept him facing that way to watch for the next possible threat. Lead whipped through the air, splitting the smoky wall and hissing as it flew over Clint's head.

The bar took most of the punishment and several rounds punched into the solid wood like hornets battering down a door. Still looking ahead of him, Clint saw something rush through the smoke as a man climbed over the bar and swung his pistol around to send a shot toward Clint's face.

When Clint saw the gun barrel swinging toward him, he let his finely honed reflexes do the rest. His arm made the proper adjustments before his finger tightened around the trigger. Less than a second before the other man took his shot, the Colt barked once and jumped in his hand.

The dirty-faced man who'd been climbing over the bar spun in the air like a hooked fish that had reached the end of its line. His face contorted and a geyser of blood exploded from the back of his head. His gun went off, but it was only because of the final contortion of his muscles; the bullet punched harmlessly into the wall.

Clint moved back into the room where he'd found Valerie, listening as the sound of the dead man's body dropping was followed by the rumble of more approaching footsteps. He wasn't sure if he'd put the leader of the men down, but he *was* sure that he hadn't heard another word come from the other end of the room.

"You all right, Valerie?" Clint asked as he continued shuffling back into the smaller room.

Taking a quick glance around, Clint wasn't able to spot the brunette right away. Before he could start thinking the worst, Valerie stuck her head out from behind a stack of crates.

"There's a door back here!" she said excitedly. "I thought I saw it before, but now I'm sure of it."

As soon as Clint was inside the smaller room, he kicked the door shut and jumped to one side. Only then did he allow himself to look away from the incoming shooters for more than a second. "Another door?"

In response to that question, Valerie pushed over a stack of crates and empty cartons to reveal a narrow door secured by a rusted metal latch. "There's only one problem," she said, pointing to a large lock hanging from the latch.

Clint motioned for her to step to one side. As soon as she was clear, he aimed the Colt and fired. Sparks flew from the lock, but the heavy device stayed right where it was. One more shot was all it took to break the lock into two pieces.

"Problem solved," he said. "Where's the door lead?"

Valerie pulled the latch aside and opened the door. She hurried up when she heard the sound of fists and boots pounding against the other door which led into the main room of the saloon. In a frenzy, she pushed open the door and practically fell through it. The rush of fresh air against her face was the answer to every hurried prayer that had been racing through her head.

"Outside!" she said gratefully. "It leads outside."

Too busy reloading his gun to share Valerie's enthusiasm, Clint said, "Then go on through and I'll be right behind you."

"You're coming, too," she said in a demanding tone that surprised even her.

Clint fired through the door, which was enough to hold back the men on the other side of it for a second or two. "I'll be right there. Just get outside and be ready to run when I come out."

That was just fine with Valerie. She ran out through the door and made sure that it was wide open before taking a look at where she'd wound up. As she'd suspected, she was in the alley between the Black Tail and its neighbor. Her heart was slamming inside her chest as she hiked up her skirts to reach for the derringer which was normally strapped to her thigh.

More prayers flew through her mind. This time, she hoped that Bret Elder hadn't found the gun when he was climbing on top of her and pitched it aside. Apparently, Clint had barged in before the other man's greasy hand had found the pistol. Thanking the Lord above as she pulled out the two-shot weapon, Valerie pointed it toward the open door and waited.

THIRTY-FOUR

Now that Valerie was clear of the room, Clint could focus more of his attention where it truly needed to be. There was no way for him to know just how many men were on the other side of the door inside the saloon. In fact, he wasn't even sure if he'd killed the one who'd shouted the order to fire or just put him down for the moment.

It had only been a few seconds since he'd gotten the main door shut, but it felt as though he'd been trapped inside the back room for hours. On a gut level, he knew his time was up. That hunch was confirmed when the banging started up again from the other side of the door and the rusty hinges started loosening from the wall.

Clint wanted to just head out through the back door and take off with Valerie in tow. The only thing stopping him from doing just that was the notion that the gunmen could just as easily chase after him. Drunk shooters like the ones filling the Black Tail might even chase after him harder if they thought he was running away from them.

There was one surefire way to discourage that type of behavior. It might not have been anything new, but Clint was certain it would work.

Backing up so that he wasn't facing the door to the

main room directly and positioning himself so he had a straight run for the back door, Clint crouched down low and kept from firing. Shots were punching holes through the door as more and more of the shooters regained their courage. A few boots slammed against the door until the whole thing busted inward, separating one set of hinges completely from the wall.

One of Clint's hands was resting on an empty crate that had been tipped over when Valerie had exposed the back door. As soon as the first shooter came stumbling into the back room, Clint tossed that crate toward the gunman with every bit of his strength.

The wooden box sailed awkwardly through the air. When he saw it coming at him, the shooter lifted one hand to protect his face and took a wild shot with the other. The gun in his hand went off and punched a hole through the crate, which wasn't enough to keep the rest of the wooden box from smashing against his head and chest.

Judging by the way the gunman hollered, one might have thought he'd been hit in the face with a shovel. It was surprise that pushed the scream out of him more than anything else, however. He was even more surprised when the men behind him fired off another volley of gunshots in response to the wild shot that had been sent into the crate.

Even Clint winced when he saw no fewer than three bullets tear through the other man's body. Two ripped through his ribs and another tore a messy hole through the man's neck, dropping him heavily to his knees.

"Holy shit," said one of the others, who was still behind the bar. "You boys just killed Marvin."

Hearing that, several sets of footsteps pounded away from the back room and went right out the front door. The ones that were left sucked up what was left of their resolve and moved forward rather than back. Marvin was either dead or well on his way when he fell flat onto the floor, clearing the line of sight for Clint as well as the other men who entered the back room.

What had started out as an expression of frightened surprise on the next man's face turned quickly into rage the moment he spotted Clint crouching near the door. A string of drunken curse words flowed from his mouth as he started lifting his gun to point it at Clint.

"Drop it," Clint said as a single warning.

Rather than do things the smart way, the drunken man took comfort from the fact that there were more men coming in from behind him and he raised his gun higher. A single shot burst inside the cramped room, which was the last thing that drunken gunman would ever hear before Clint's bullet dug a tunnel through his skull.

Without missing a beat, Clint aimed carefully at the next man and squeezed off another shot. That one whipped through the air and tore a chunk out of the man's cheek. The gunman that was next in line to enter the room reeled back as blood sprayed from the injured man's wound, and a loud, agonizing scream exploded from the depths of his lungs.

Clint couldn't help but smile. Although the shot appeared to be messy, that was exactly what he'd wanted. The man's wound, while not fatal, was messy and bloody. Thanks to the man's dramatic carrying on, blood sprayed out into a wide arc as he swung his entire body toward the other men crowding around behind him. Flaps of torn skin wagged outward as he moved.

All in all, it was one hell of a show and the wounded man himself couldn't have done anything more to enhance the performance. There was blood everywhere and as soon as the others saw what had happened to their friend, they suddenly lost their desire to come into the room after Clint.

"What the hell's wrong with you?" came the familiar

voice of Randal Elder from the saloon's main room. "Go on in there or I won't pay you shit!"

Clint could hear several sets of footsteps moving back, as well as one more deep voice that sounded only partially sober.

"Go in there yourself," the half-drunk voice said. "This ain't worth what you're payin'."

Nodding while inching back toward the smaller door, Clint was glad his little discouragement had worked. While he would have been perfectly able to fight his way through those men, it sat a whole lot better with him to get them to leave on their own.

As much as he wanted to get through the others, Randal was impeded by the drunks trying to go the other way as well as the man with the facial wound who stumbled around like a freshly decapitated chicken. Finally, Randal got close enough to take a look through the door to the back room. He saw a brief glimpse of Clint stepping through the rear exit before another shot was fired in Randal's direction.

The bullet wound in his shoulder was still fresh and Randal nearly tripped over himself backpedaling away from the narrow door. "Aw, to hell with it," Randal grunted. "Let 'em go. That dumb bitch already paid me my money anyhow."

That was music to Clint's ears.

THIRTY-FIVE

Just to be on the safe side, he slammed the door shut the moment he stepped outside. As luck would have it, the remains of the latch wedged against the door frame to hold the entire wooden panel in place. For a brief second when he turned around, Clint thought that he wasn't half as lucky as he'd thought.

When he spotted Valerie standing with one shoulder against the building, Clint's eyes darted straight to the little gun clutched in her fist. He could sight right down the wrong end of the barrel to tell that she was aiming the weapon straight at him.

"Don't sh—" was all Clint managed to say before the derringer spat out its tongue of smoke and spark.

The small caliber round hissed through space, missing Clint's ear by an inch or so. It continued down to the front of the alley and dug into the upper chest of the man who'd been coming around the corner drawing a bead on Clint's back.

While the .22 round might not have packed too much punch behind it, there was more than enough to cause some hurt and make the gunman stop short before pulling his own trigger. More than that, Valerie gave Clint enough

140

time to spin around and bring the Colt up to bear on the man who'd been a second away from ambushing him.

Seeing that he'd lost the element of surprise and feeling the new chunk of lead in his body, the other gunman tossed down his weapon and turned to run in the opposite direction. He disappeared in the blink of an eye and didn't seem all too anxious to make a second appearance.

Clint holstered the Colt and turned away from the front of the alley as well. Breaking into a run, he grabbed hold of Valerie's arm as he raced by her. "Thanks," he said as she raced to keep up with him.

"You didn't think I was gonna leave you in there did you?"

"No, but I was hoping you would have at least gotten a little farther away from that hornet's nest."

She shook her head and grinned smugly. "Not after all you've done for me. I heard a lot of shooting. Did you kill all those men that were in that place?"

"I only shot the ones I had to. I've already got my share of ghosts haunting me."

Valerie let out a tired breath that had nothing to do with the quick pace of her steps. "So they'll be coming after us?" she asked.

Despite everything that was happening, Clint had to let out a little laugh when he heard that question. Mainly that was because he could still picture the terrified expression on some of those faces as well as the melodramatic reaction of the one who'd taken a scrape to the cheek. "I don't think we have to worry about that. One thing's for sure," he added as they ran out of the alley and came out behind the row of buildings, "you definitely shouldn't go back into that saloon anytime soon."

"That's another thing we don't have to worry about. Trust me on that."

Clint paused just long enough to spot another alleyway which connected to the buildings one street over from the

Black Tail Saloon. Still keeping hold of Valerie's arm, he jogged across one back lot and entered the next alley. Clint took some care going down that cramped space, making sure that he wasn't about to charge into another ambush.

It didn't take long for him to realize that not only wasn't there anyone ahead of them, but also there wasn't even anyone running up on them from behind. The second alley opened up onto a fairly crowded street and the people walking on either side of it apparently hadn't heard any of the gunshots.

Either that, or the sound of shooting coming from the Black Tail Saloon wasn't anything new to the locals.

Clint glanced quickly right and then left, which was enough to satisfy him that they weren't in immediate danger. All of the folks walking down the boardwalks were minding their own business and didn't take much notice of him or Valerie at all. Although Valerie had done a fine job of keeping up with Clint before, she seemed real glad to slow down for a bit now.

As they stepped onto the boardwalk, Clint let go of her elbow and almost immediately felt Valerie slide her arm around his. To the rest of the world, they looked like just another couple out for a stroll. In fact, both of them felt their hearts racing within their chests and it was a struggle to slow their breathing down to a more manageable pace.

"So what do we do now?" Valerie asked as soon as she caught her breath.

Clint gave a friendly nod to someone walking by and said, "I need to fetch my things and then get my horse. After that, we leave this place."

"We?"

"Yep. You're coming with me. Is that a problem?"

"What if I said it was?"

"Then I'd just have to remind you about the professional assassin who wanted to kill you and missed," Clint said, still maintaining his casual tone of voice. "I know you don't know a lot about those kind of men, but one thing's for damn sure: they don't like to miss."

"And where do we go?"

"I've got a place in mind, but it would be better if I didn't say much while we're still in town."

"What's the matter?" Valerie asked in a semi-teasing way. "Afraid someone's listening in on us from the shadows?"

"I'm not sure, but I wouldn't rule that out." Clint let that sink in mainly just to get Valerie back in a serious frame of mind. "It's just that I'll be a whole lot more comfortable when we're out of here and that assassin is out of the picture."

"Are you going to track him down?"

"Looks like I'll have to and you'll have to come with me. It's the only way I can keep you safe."

"So how do you find this killer if he's already gone?" Valerie asked. "Doesn't he already have a head start on us?"

"I know who his next target's going to be, which is all I need to find him."

"Are you sure this is the best thing to do? I mean, he might kill us both if he sees us again."

Clint looked at her and said, "After what happened here, this town is too dangerous for you and I can't stay here knowing that killer is putting someone else in his sights. When there's no turning back, that only leaves one other option."

"Yeah," Valerie said. "Straight ahead."

THIRTY-SIX

Luckily for Clint, the ambush at the Black Tail Saloon was like a fire that had been properly contained. It had raged hot and burned itself out quickly, but didn't spread much farther from where it had started. That was pretty much the way Clint had figured it to be since the look in the gunmen's eyes was mostly drunken anger instead of intense murderous rage. If one of those shooters saw Clint walking down the street, he would probably just let him go rather than start any more trouble.

Clint was a bit concerned about the price put on his head, but he would ask Valerie about that later. After all, it was only a hundred dollars. If those men in the Black Tail had been sober, they probably would have laughed at the offer instead of put their lives on the line to reach for it.

Doing their best to not draw any more attention to themselves, Clint and Valerie made a stop at Monroe's as well as Valerie's home so they could each collect their belongings. Valerie was too distracted to think about leaving most of her things behind and didn't put up much of a fight when Clint hurried her along.

In less than an hour, they were putting the saddle on

Eclipse's back and loading up their things. The Darley Arabian bristled under the added weight, but didn't have any trouble carrying it. More than anything, the stallion was just glad to be out of the confines of the stable and heading for the open trail.

The truth of the matter was that Clint really didn't know if there was anyone else watching him either from the government or Meers himself. There could be any number of spies keeping track of him and Valerie. Then again, there could be nobody. Since Clint wasn't much for unanswered questions that could affect his life, he decided to keep his eyes open and figure that there was good reason to be careful.

They rode out of Port Saunders easily and with pleasant looks on their faces. Even if there were no spies tracking them, he kept up their easygoing appearance so they gave none of the locals anything to remember them by. Like just another leaf that dropped from a tree in the autumn, they left town and surely wouldn't be missed.

If anyone asked about them, there would be nothing much to recall. If experienced watchers were keeping up with them, they would at least be under the impression that Clint was in no particular hurry.

Most of the day passed with Clint watching the landscape as he steered Eclipse toward their next destination. In his head, he plotted out the path they would take very carefully to make absolutely sure that they were heading for the speediest course.

There was some serious riding ahead of them and, for Eclipse's sake, he didn't want to start off going too fast. The stallion was young and strong, but he was also carrying a heavier load. After a few days of rest, breaking into a hard gallop bearing twice the amount he was used to could very well injure the Darley Arabian. After what had happened in Texas, Clint didn't want to see Eclipse hurt again anytime soon.

Behind him, Valerie sat with both arms wrapped around Clint's midsection and her head resting upon his back. Her fingers were locked tightly in place, and she drifted in and out of sleep for the first several hours of the ride. Everything that had happened recently caught up to her in a rush until it was a chore just to keep her eyes open.

There was plenty she wanted to ask Clint, but she simply didn't have the energy. Not just then, anyway. For the moment, it was all she could do to stay upright while drifting in and out of an uneasy sleep. Besides, Clint didn't appear to be in a talkative mood anyhow.

Every so often, Clint could feel her body slipping a little too far in one direction. He would reach back and keep her from slipping off, which also woke her up and tightened her grip around him. When the sun started slipping toward the western horizon, Clint flicked Eclipse's reins so they could get a little more distance before it was too late to keep riding.

They'd been heading south and southeast all day. As they rode, the smell of the ocean became more and more faint and the air took on just a bit more of the summer's weight. Although Port Saunders was a port in name only, it had been close enough to the ocean for a man to feel the wide open waters on his face and breathe it in whenever he filled his lungs.

The ocean was still present in the wind, but only as a recent memory. The trees were becoming thicker around the trail they'd been riding, which made it easier to find a suitable place to set up camp. Clint passed up a few more obvious choices in favor of someplace that would offer them cover while allowing him to watch for anyone riding up on them.

Valerie was grateful to climb down from the saddle and took a few moments to stretch her legs. It had been the first time they'd stopped for more than a minute or two and she found herself walking a little farther away than she'd intended.

"Don't wander off now," Clint said, his arms full of firewood. "I'd hate to have to ride all the way back to Port Saunders to pick you up."

She smirked at the sound of the town's name. "Why would I go back there? It already sounds like someplace I barely remember."

Putting down the firewood and forming it into a pyramid over some kindling, Clint took some flint from his saddlebag and brought a little sputtering flame to life. "You'll be able to go back," he said while nursing the fire along. "Once this mess is cleared up, there's no reason why you shouldn't have your normal life again."

Shaking her head, Valerie couldn't keep from laughing. "Normal life? The sad thing is that getting pinned down by sweaty pigs and ducking the occasional bullet is normal for me."

"And here I thought you made your living cheating at cards."

"Cheating?"

Clint nodded while keeping his friendly smile intact. "That and stealing from the men you share your bed with."

Valerie looked offended and stayed that way as Clint walked up to her and slid his hands around her waist. That offended look faded a bit when he slipped his hands into the pockets of her skirts and came out with a folded bundle of cash.

Flipping over the bundle of money, Clint revealed an engraving etched upon the metal clip. The engraving revealed his own initials. "Come on over to the fire," he said. "We need to talk."

THIRTY-SEVEN

The line of wagons traveling together didn't look like much. Of course, that was just so long as whoever was doing the looking didn't know what to look for. There were five wagons in all, but only three stuck together at any given time. The rest were spread out over a quarter of a mile or so at the most, but usually stuck a little closer together than that.

Each of the wagons appeared to be full and most of the men riding in them appeared to be armed. They wore holsters and carried rifles as well as shotguns at all times.

The wagons were fully loaded and pulled by a team of fine looking horses which were well cared for and never pushed too close to their physical limits.

All of this was what could be seen by anyone watching the caravan for more than an hour or so. None of this gave away much more than what the drivers of the caravan planned to give away.

Unfortunately for those drivers, there was someone watching them who was anything but a casual observer.

The rider had caught up to the caravan after a full day's ride. He'd pushed himself so hard in getting there that he'd nearly collapsed several times under all the stress.

His eyelids were lead curtains being held up by nothing more than an iron will. Even his breathing was labored and only the strictest of self-control kept his heart from giving out.

No matter how much practiced concentration the rider could exert over himself, he was unable to maintain such control over his horse. The mare that had carried Adam Meers out of Port Saunders was on its last breaths close to the end of his journey. Meers overtook another traveler and stole his horse just minutes before his original ride keeled over.

Now, Meers allowed his new horse to take it a little easier since he had his target in sight. He was able to pick out many more details from the caravan of wagons with only a few hours to watch it. Of course, it helped having plenty of information about the caravan prior even to when he'd put down Martin Smythe.

Just knowing the importance of the caravan's main passenger was enough to tip off the assassin as to what he should expect from everyone within the other wagons. First of all, he knew that the row of wagons wasn't just another caravan moving together because they shared a common destination.

Those wagons made up an armed convoy.

From the scouting Meers had already done, he knew that the target he was after was in one of those wagons. It was impossible for him to be sure of which one because they were all heavily guarded. He knew he was going to have to get a much closer look before he could narrow down his killing field any more.

The man who'd given him his assignment had already told him that one of those wagons was set up as a decoy to throw off any possible assassination attempts. After what had happened to Smythe, it was very possible that yet another decoy was among the convoy as well.

Meers didn't need to be told that there would be more

guards than he could see from where he was. Common sense would tell anyone that there would be other gunmen within the wagons and possibly at the towns along the way to guard someone as important as the convoy's main passenger. Meers also knew those gunmen wouldn't just be ordinary guards either. They would be experienced soldiers ready to lay down their lives to protect the man at the center of that convoy.

Not even the slightest crack formed in the assassin's mental armor when he considered the possibility that one of those guards could very well be someone he knew personally. Professional killers weren't the most social of creatures, but they worked in certain tight circles of comrades.

Unlike most other circles of friends, killers knew early on that they couldn't really trust anyone. Not even each other. Deep down inside their souls, the thought of killing one of their few friends was regrettable, but not impossible.

So far, Meers hadn't seen any familiar faces, but that didn't mean they weren't there. In fact, if there were guards there who he might consider a comrade, odds were that he wouldn't see them at all until the moment of truth.

When the moment of truth was reached, there would be no turning back. That was the solemn truth for this as well as any other job.

It was a truth Adam Meers lived by.

It was a truth he would die by.

All of that flowed through the back of his mind while the rest of his thoughts were occupied with hundreds of other more important factors. He studied the speed of the convoy, the alertness of the guards, the number of passengers, as well as the amount of guns he could see. Every second, he calculated wind speed and the movement of both himself as well as the wagons to figure the shot he would take at any single moment.

Every part of him was preparing to take a life; several lives if necessary.

He'd been in that frame of mind for so long that Meers practically forgot what it was like to close his eyes all the way or truly savor a night's sleep. After years of taking jobs or waiting for the next one, Meers had become a machine. Instead of steam, he ran on pure force of will and his body moved just as surely as the pistons of a train's engine.

Early on in his career, he'd put aside the notions of right and wrong. None of that mattered anymore.

All that did matter was that he perform his duty and become the best at what he did. Watching the convoy roll carefully onward and tracking the movements of all the armed guards, Meers took no small amount of pride from the fact that he'd gotten as close as he was. That pride would swell within his chest when he saw the guards watch helplessly as his target fell.

Even though Meers knew he might not walk away from that job, he had no doubt that he would see it through. That assignment, much like the course of his life, was too far along for him to choose another path.

He was a killer. His heart was cold. His body was a machine. His soul was damned.

There was no turning back.

THIRTY-EIGHT

Even as she saw the money clip that had been found in the secret pocket of her skirt, Valerie put on a convincing innocent face. She stuck out her bottom lip to pout ever so slightly and bowed her head as though she was truly afraid Clint might strike her.

For a moment, Clint found himself actually feeling guilty for having been the cause of such a face. He wondered if he'd been too harsh when calling her out for what she'd done or if he'd been too gruff with her after they'd shared such a trying couple of days.

Then, he came to his senses.

"You've been stealing from me," he said as a simple statement of fact.

She accentuated the pout a bit more and looked away slightly. "Just a little."

When he felt the first onset of a sympathetic reaction, Clint shook his head and said, "Don't pull this crap with me, Valerie. Did you cheat at cards, too?"

Clint asked that second question only as a test. Since he already knew the answer, he thought he'd get a look at how she would react when she replied.

Without missing a beat or batting an eyelash, Valerie

straightened herself up and looked truly offended. "Cheat at cards? Clint Adams, I do not have to cheat at cards. And I thought you'd be the last one to be such a sore loser. Just because I might have had a run or two of good l—"

"I know you cheated," Clint interrupted.

She froze with her mouth about to form the rest of her word. Slowly, she let her muscles relax and lowered her head once more. "Oh. Now you think I'm a liar, too?"

"No. I think you're used to talking your way out of things rather than fighting your way out."

"Then why try to save my life?" she asked with the threat of tears imposing behind her words. "If I'm such a bad person, why not just let me get killed?"

Rolling his eyes, Clint dropped himself onto the ground beside the fire. "Jesus, Valerie, you can cut the drama. I'm not in the mood for it."

"Then you're not mad at me?" she asked hopefully.

"Not as such. I've been around long enough to know that cheating isn't anything personal."

Now she was starting to look a little confused. "Are you going to turn me in to the law?"

Clint laughed at that. "Why would I do that? The law in Port Saunders that isn't related to you is about as useful as tits on a bull."

"Then why bring it up?"

"Because I wanted my money back."

Clint's last statement hung in the air for a second or two as the fire started to pop and crackle between them. Finally, both he and Valerie broke into laughter that went on a little longer than needed simply because it was such a good release after such a hard day.

By the time they caught their breath, Valerie had moved around the fire and was sitting with her back leaning against Clint's chest. She leaned her head against him as well and let out a soothing breath.

"I wanted to help you," she said, staring up at the blanket of stars shimmering over them. "When I went into that saloon to look for Addy, I really wanted to find out something that would help you."

"I know."

"I'm just sorry I couldn't do anything but get myself into a fix where you had to come and pull me out again."

"To tell you the truth, I'm glad I could be there for you. And besides that, you did help me."

She sat up and turned around. The sparkle in her eyes was almost as bright as the stars they'd both been admiring. "Really?"

"Yes. On both counts."

"So how did I help you by getting myself pinned beneath that pig of an Elder?"

"Well," Clint said as he shifted his weight to a more comfortable position. "I knew that Meers wouldn't just leave town without making sure his witnesses were taken care of."

"Meers. Is that the assassin's name?"

"Yeah. Adam Meers. You ever hear that name before?"

She thought about it for a second or two before shaking her head.

Clint would have been more surprised if she'd said she *had* heard of him. Either way, it really didn't matter. "Anyhow, Meers was either going to take care of us himself or have someone else do it for him. By walking into that ambush, it put my mind at ease to know that he'd passed off the job of killing us for the time being."

"That made you feel better, huh? Getting shot at didn't quite have the same effect on me."

"Well let's put it this way. Would you rather get shot at by a bunch of drunks or by a professional killer?"

This time, Valerie didn't have to think about anything before she answered. "I see your point. So where did Meers get off to?"

"That's what I talked about with Mr. Marsden," Clint said. "He told me a whole lot about this Meers fellow and why he might want to kill that Englishman."

Clint took a few moments to tell Valerie about the basics of what he'd learned from the Secret Service man. He didn't have to be told by Marsden that most of what had been said was strictly confidential, so he filled her in on only the basic facts that directly concerned their situation.

She listened intently as the expression on her face became more and more dark. After all, it didn't take an expert to know when a situation was about to go from bad to worse.

"So this is something to do with the war?" she asked. "But that's been over for more than twenty years."

"That doesn't matter. At least not to some people. There was a whole lot more at stake than just slaves and land. There were power struggles and plenty of money to be made."

"And plenty of money to be lost."

Clint nodded. "I knew you'd be able to relate to that."

"Sure. High stakes are high stakes. So where do we fit in?"

"Unfortunately, as of the moment when we got involved with the Englishman's death, we fit right into the middle of this whole thing. Meers is going after someone else and I was asked to stop him."

"Can't you just say no to the whole thing?"

"I could, but what fun would that be?" This time, it was Clint who tried to ease the tension by putting on a fake smile. Valerie bought into it just as much as he did when the smirk was on the other face.

"Look," he said, shaking off the attempt at humor. "I may not be familiar with Hugh Marsden, but I worked a couple of times with the agency that sent him, and I have a good friend there. He's been there to pull my fat out of the fire a few times and I owe him a favor. This'll be my way of paying him back. Besides, this is a job that's worth doing no matter who's asking."

"What is it, Clint? Where are we going?"

"We're headed for Fresno, but we'll probably see some action before we get there. A man's on his way to a meeting there involving several international politicians who've climbed up the ladder considerably since the war."

"Anyone I might have heard of?" Valerie asked innocently.

"At least one. The president."

THIRTY-NINE

Valerie's face froze when Clint said who was next on the assassin's list. Then she let her eyes drift down to the fire as the weight of what she'd heard sank in.

"The president?" she asked out of disbelief. "You mean . . . our president?"

"This country's president, that's right."

"Oh my God."

"That's pretty much what I said."

"Are you sure about this?"

Clint turned to face the fire as well and started keeping his hands busy by preparing a small meal. "I read about this meeting in Fresno not too long ago in the newspapers. Having a killer after someone that high up explains a lot. Like why Meers was in such a hurry to leave us and move on to his next target, for example. It also explains why the Secret Service sent an agent to meet with me so quickly and why they're so insistent that I take the job myself. The Service isn't in the business of asking for help unless it's truly needed."

"Well, I guess this sure as hell qualifies."

Nodding, Clint held a frying pan over the fire and warmed up some strips of bacon and beans. On any other night, the fresh air and the smell of cooking food would have been comforting. On that night, however, there wasn't much that could untie the knot in the middle of Clint's stomach.

"There's still plenty about this that bothers me," Clint said, thinking out loud. "According to Marsden, this assassin was told to kill these men during the war. I know a lot could have happened to postpone the job. If the targets found out what was happening, they could have gone into hiding or even sent out their own men to keep them under protection.

"But like you said, that was over twenty years ago. Any assassin worth his salt wouldn't take that long to kill his target unless he was called off the job."

"But if he was called off," Valerie said, picking up where Clint had stopped. "Then someone must have told him to go after these men again, right?"

"Yeah," Clint said, even though it tied that knot in his stomach even tighter. "That's exactly right."

"Who would do something like that?"

Clint shrugged and shook his head. "The sad part is that there's no shortage of people who would do something like this. The real question is who would have the power to actually pull this off. Marsden didn't say anything about it in particular, but I know it's got to be someone in the government that's pulling Meers's strings."

"If that's the case, what are we supposed to do about it?" Valerie asked. She stared into the fire as though she were watching something happen within the flames while her mind went through all of the bad things she was hearing. "I mean, what if there's even more going on that we don't know about? What if that agent you talked to was a part of this and is sending us into a trap?"

Her eyes widened a bit more and she set her chin down on top of her knees. "What if there's a killer like this Meers person after us already?"

"Well, if it makes you feel any better, Meers is already after us and we're still alive and kicking."

"Maybe, but for how much longer?"

"As long as we stay one step ahead of the game," Clint replied with nothing but confidence in his voice. Reaching out, he put a hand on her shoulder and gently turned her so that he could look into her eyes. "This is just like a poker game, Valerie. Believe me. I know what I'm talking about. I get killers coming after me just because of who I am."

As good a con artist as she might have been, Valerie wasn't able to show anything but her true feelings at that particular moment. Clint could tell that much just by looking at her. She was scared to the verge of tears. Clint was sure of it.

"I'm good at poker," she said, trying to keep her chin up.

"Then you know that every little piece of information you can get about who you're playing against could very well make the difference between winning and losing. Meers can't know that we're still alive. And my gut tells me that he won't know we're after him right now, either."

"So you think Marsden is trustworthy?"

"I wouldn't go that far, but I'm fairly certain he's playing on the right side. If he wasn't, he would have tried to kill one or both of us already. Sending drunks in after someone isn't exactly a professional's style."

Valerie nodded. "I guess so."

"Now for this to work at all, I'll need you to trust me and do as I say," Clint told her. He held her gaze and stared at her intensely, studying every inch of her that might tip him off to whether or not she was holding something back. "Do you trust me?"

"I was almost raped in that back room," she said. "You came and got me out of there. I might have been killed in that same room when all those drunks started shooting, but you got me out of there. I would have been dead for sure if Meers had a few more seconds with me. I'm sure of it. You got me out of there as well.

"What I'm trying to say is that I trust you and I owe you, Clint Adams. And whatever you need to do, I want to help you do it. So you damn well better not be thinking of dropping me off somewhere before riding on to Fresno."

Clint wasn't going to let her out of his sight simply because he was fairly certain that she would be dead within a day or two if he did. But rather than tell her that, he nodded and accepted what she'd said. She was scared enough already. There was no use in pushing her any further.

"All right," he said. "We'll both ride out tomorrow good and early. Before sunrise, even. The only reason I stopped and made camp at all was to give Eclipse a chance to rest up. Tomorrow, he'll be getting pushed to his limit for most of the day."

"You think we'll get there in time?"

"Honestly, I don't know. For now, we can only do what we can do."

"Play the cards we were dealt, huh?" Valerie pointed out with a wary smile. "This is a lot like poker."

FORTY

Nobody who didn't have an important job in the United States government knew who was riding in that convoy of wagons. The meeting in Fresno was known, but for security, the president's route and exact arrival time were kept under wraps. For that reason, the convoy stopped outside of a small town less than a half-day's ride from Fresno so that guards could ride in and fetch supplies while the president stayed behind.

The accommodations weren't exactly what the leader of the country was used to, but they were tolerable under the circumstances. Secret Service men and soldiers alike went about their duties like bees swarming around their hive while scouts and the cook rode on ahead.

Horseback patrols circled the wagons as well from a wider distance. They made sure nobody was following the procession or trying to get a closer look. There were no uniforms visible and not one official marking to be seen, although the men wore matching red armbands and dark bandannas to act as markings that could be seen from a distance. To anyone who somehow managed to get a look at the wagons, it would seem like just a busier-than-

normal wagon train carrying possibly an important busi-
nessman or two.

Adam Meers watched all of the activity from a distance
that was closer than he thought he might have gotten.
Despite the efforts of the patrols, the men on horseback
were soldiers and therefore very predictable. They rode in
easily recognizable patterns and in shifts that the assassin
could set his clock by. In fact, he had set his watch to
them and used it as a tool to predict when the patrol would
be coming near him again.

For the moment, he was safe. Keeping his horse teth-
ered a quarter of a mile away, he'd limped in closer on
foot until he found a spot that suited his needs perfectly.
There wasn't a lot of hiding spaces to choose from, which
was why the soldiers had chosen it to stop and give the
horses a rest. The trail stretched out for miles in either
direction with little or no cover on either side except for
a few thin trees and some sparse clumps of bushes.

The grade of the land rose and fell slightly. It wasn't
much more than a slight, jagged incline, but it was enough
to form little dents and ridges in the earth. Meers didn't
choose the largest ridge or the smallest one, but picked
one of the average-sized ones instead. Those were the
ones that would attract less attention and blend in easier
with the surrounding terrain.

He stretched out upon uncomfortable ground in a position that contorted his body in some odd angles. He
wasn't concerned about comfort or even the pain he felt
from his joints and back. All that mattered was that he
was both flat against the ground and still able to watch
the convoy and nearby patrols.

Craning his neck until he thought he might just snap
it out of joint himself, Meers looked toward the sound of
approaching horses. A patrol consisting of two mounted
soldiers was headed straight toward his position. There
was no mistaking the military precision of their riding

style or the perfectly straight posture maintained while in the saddle.

Meers's finger tightened slightly around the trigger of the rifle in his hands, but otherwise remained perfectly still. Just to make sure he didn't give himself away by any unwanted glare from the moon or stars, he lowered his eyelids until he was peeking out from between the lashes.

Every muscle was prepared to move at a moment's notice but for the time being, he was just another motionless formation amid the rippling sea of dirt, sand and rock.

Although they'd been riding on patrol for over three hours, neither of the two men on horseback had spoken more than a dozen or so words to each other. Those few that had been said were nothing more than orders and acknowledgement of those orders. They were too busy doing their duty to say anything more.

Although both men appeared to be staring straight ahead, they both stopped in perfect unison when the shorter of the two men lifted his left hand with his palm facing forward. The horses responded like the well-trained workers they were and waited patiently for their next command.

The man who'd given the signal to stop sat low in the saddle due to a squat, thick torso. His arms were covered in leathery muscle which stretched all the way up his shoulders and wrapped around his neck. Simple features stood out on his clean-shaven face. Dark eyes gazed out from beneath a furrowed brow and bald head.

Riding next to the bald man was a younger man with an equally muscled build. Even though he was taller than his partner, it was plain to see that he knew he wasn't the bald man's equal. Like the horses, the younger man sat and waited to be told what to do.

"Did you see that?" the bald man asked.

After a second to take another look around, the younger man replied, "See what, Sergeant Velasco?"

Still holding his left hand up, the sergeant curled all his fingers down except for one. He used that finger to point toward the area directly in front of them.

The younger man followed that finger and looked where he was directed. He hadn't seen anything worth stopping for previously, and he still didn't even after giving the land another glance. "I don't see anything, sir."

Sergeant Velasco heard what the other man said, but didn't give any outward sign. Instead, he stared at the ground in front of him, certain that there was something he was missing.

The terrain was slightly uneven and had its share of ruts, cracks and bumps, but there didn't seem to be anything else. If there was anything an experienced soldier trusted, it was his own senses and instincts. Velasco hadn't stopped for no reason, but he simply couldn't nail down what it was that had caught his attention.

After a minute had passed in silence, the other rider said, "Sir? Should I bring some reinforcements?"

"No. It was probably just a coyote."

"Probably, sir. They're all over the place."

Even as they snapped their reins and rode away, it was obvious that Velasco wasn't satisfied with his own assessment. He just hadn't been able to come up with a better one. The younger soldier saw it on his sergeant's face.

Meers had seen it, too.

FORTY-ONE

"So what else did you two talk about?"

Sitting next to the fire and warming up a pot of coffee to wash down the dinner he'd prepared, Clint looked up at Valerie and asked, "Who are you talking about?"

"You and that government man, Marsden. Was there anything else he told you?"

Not for the first time since he'd been in her company, Clint got the distinctive feeling that Valerie was digging for information. Seeing as how her life was in danger and she'd been dragged out of her own town, she did have good reason to want to know all she could. On the other hand, there was something about her tone of voice that just didn't sit right with Clint sometimes.

"He told me the route the president is taking into Fresno, but I practically had to drag that out of him with a team of mules."

"Really? What else?"

Clint wasn't even tempted to go into any more detail. Most of that was because of the promise he'd made to Marsden when he'd talked to the Secret Service man in the first place. There was also that little bit of something else which made Clint hold his tongue.

"I'm not in the Secret Service, Valerie. That's reason enough for Marsden to keep a whole lot from me."

"Oh, I know. Just thought I'd see if there was anything else I could help you with."

"You've done plenty for me already," Clint assured her. "Just get some rest. You're going to need it."

For the next couple of minutes, the only sound that could be heard was the rustle of the wind and the crackle of the fire as it chewed on the wood Clint had gathered. The silence wasn't uncomfortable, but it did hang between Clint and Valerie like a thin curtain.

Each person could see through to the other side, but there was no mistaking the fact that a barrier was indeed between them.

By scooting forward just an inch or so, Valerie was able to get close enough to feel the heat of Clint's breath as he exhaled. She could feel the heat from his body as well but most importantly, she felt that she'd broken the thin wall that had sprung up in the space of a few minutes.

"There," she said, nuzzling her cheek against his. "That's a whole lot better."

Clint responded to the feel of her skin against his, but didn't take his eyes from the fire. He could also feel her hand resting on his thigh, working its way up until it stopped just short of his groin. She massaged his muscles with slow, strong fingers; the sound of her breathing speeding up in his ear.

"Can I ask you something, Clint?"

"Sure. Go right ahead."

"Why did you save me?"

That question wasn't at all what he'd expected. In fact, it struck him as downright peculiar. "What are you talking about?"

Keeping one hand on his thigh, Valerie used her other hand to reach up and turn Clint's face gently until she could look directly into his eyes. "You know what kind of woman I was. You obviously know what kind of woman I am and . . . how I stole from you. Most men would want to shoot me themselves, not to mention risk their lives getting me out of that snake pit at the Black Tail.

"Why would you do something like that?" she asked again earnestly. "I mean, I'm grateful and all, but you hardly know me."

Clint smiled at her and placed his hand on top of the one resting upon his thigh. "Just because you stole some money from me and tried to cheat me at cards doesn't mean I want to see you dead. Part of gambling is reading people. I know you're a good woman underneath it all."

Her eyes had widened just a bit, but it was enough for Clint to notice.

"You knew about that?" she asked.

"About you being a good person? Yeah. It was something in your eyes."

"No. I mean about me cheating you at cards. You knew?"

Laughing, Clint nodded. "I've sat across the table from some of the best card players and cheats in the world. You're slick, Valerie, but not that slick."

Although slightly embarrassed at having been found out, Valerie rolled her eyes, but kept both hands on Clint. She moved a little closer, placing her lips so that they brushed against Clint's mouth like butterfly wings when she spoke.

"Then maybe I need to work on distracting you a little better," she whispered.

"Why's that?" Clint asked, pretending that he didn't know exactly what she was doing or what she really wanted. "Are you planning on asking me for a rematch?"

Valerie moved around so that she sat between Clint and the fire. She straddled his outstretched legs and settled herself down so that her breasts were pressed tightly against his chest. "Cards weren't exactly on my mind, but I was thinking about giving something else another go."

"And what might that be?"

Sliding her hand up along Clint's thigh, Valerie slipped her fingers between his legs and cupped the growing bulge waiting for her there. All it took was another gentle massage for her to coax him into a full erection.

"I think you know damn well what I'm talking about, Clint Adams."

"Really? Well if you're so good at reading people, let's put you to the test." With that, Clint used both hands to feel the strong, tight muscles in her legs. His fingers slid beneath the material of her skirts and traced a line along the backs of her knees.

Valerie sucked in a deep breath and closed her eyes as she felt his touch moving along her thighs until finally his hands were cupping her buttocks. Lifting up just enough to let his hands go farther, she let out a breath and leaned back as Clint's fingertips drifted dangerously close to the moist lips of her vagina.

"All right now," Clint said. "Tell me. What do I want right now?"

Almost immediately, Valerie started tugging at his belt and unfastening his jeans. As soon as she had his cock free, she stroked it and began nibbling at the base of his neck.

"Damn," Clint said in a strained whisper. "You're good."

FORTY-TWO

The stars stretched out overhead.

The fire crackled and popped to Clint's side.

All around him, he could feel the cool night air flowing by, gently stroking his skin as it passed in much the same way that Valerie's hands gently stroked his shoulders and neck. Directly in front of him, all Clint could see was Valerie's face and naked body, rising and falling to a steady, insistent rhythm as she rode up and down on his cock.

She straddled him, her palms braced against his chest so she could control the speed of her lovemaking while allowing Clint's hands to roam freely over her body. The upper portion of her dress was pulled down and her skirts were bunched up around her waist, falling behind her like a thin curtain of material.

The light of the fire framed her beautifully, making the clothing that hung down from her waist seem more like a backdrop instead of anything attached to her. Clint rubbed one hand along her leg, feeling the muscles moving as she rode him with a subtle forward and backward shift that rubbed her clitoris along the shaft of his penis. When she did that, Valerie let out a soft moan that drifted out and was immediately swallowed up by the wind.

Clint's other hand traveled up her side; his fingers sliding over her bare ribs and his thumb drifting first over her stomach and then along the side of her breast. All the while, he watched her move. He watched the look on her face change whenever she found a new way to turn or he pushed his hips up a bit or a little to the side.

Valerie had her hands on her knees, squatting down on top of him before moving her fingers up her thigh and between her legs. It sent an excited chill through both of them as she began to shamelessly pleasure herself by rubbing her clitoris while taking him all the way inside.

As Clint watched, he felt his own body craving her more. Even though he was already inside her, he still felt like that wasn't enough. He put both hands on her hips and squeezed her buttocks, guiding her to bounce faster on top of him while he began thrusting upward with growing force.

Whenever he pushed up into her harder, Clint felt her body tense and heard her moans become louder and more passionate. Soon, she was the one keeping still while he pumped into her from below. She leaned forward and placed her palms on his chest for support, arching her back while tossing her dark hair over her shoulders.

All Clint had to do was sit up a little bit for Valerie to know what he wanted from her. Responding to the motions of his body, she climbed off of him and settled onto the ground while Clint got to his knees and moved closer.

They could feel the warmth of the fire on one side, contrasting sharply to the bite of cold air on the other. Kneeling while facing each other, they embraced and kissed passionately in the open air, their hands wandering freely over the other's body while pressing as close together as they could possibly get.

Clint's rigid penis rubbed between her thighs and although Valerie spread her legs to feel him press against her vagina, she moaned impatiently when he didn't slip immediately inside. For a bit, they enjoyed the carnal torture of getting so close to penetration, but always being denied.

The lips of her pussy were wet and warm and Clint savored the way they felt against his thick column of flesh. Once his hands got back onto her hips, however, he pushed her away and turned her around. He couldn't wait any longer and by the quick way Valerie followed his lead, she was feeling the same.

With her back to him, Valerie reached around until she felt her fingers slide through Clint's hair. They were still kneeling, but now Clint was able to reach around and cup both of her breasts in his hands. Valerie's nipples were small and hard and she moaned louder when he pinched them gently between thumb and forefinger.

He slid his hands over her breasts once more and then eased them along her sides. Just as his thumbs ran over the base of her spine, she leaned forward until she was on all fours with her chest close to the ground and her backside lifted slightly in the air.

It was as though Clint's body found its way inside of her on its own. His own hardness was enough for the tip of his cock to slide between her thighs and enter the wet opening of her pussy. From there, Clint took hold of her waist and pulled her toward him while thrusting inside.

Their bodies came together so perfectly that the sensation nearly overtook them both. Clint's entire length eased inside of her until his waist pushed up against her buttocks. Pushing just a little farther into her, Clint brought a cry of pleasure from Valerie's lips that echoed loudly into the night.

She dug her fingers into the dirt and tossed her hair back as he started to move in and out of her. When she wanted it harder, all she had to do was push herself back at the right moment and Clint pounded into her with just the right amount of force. Soon, her hair was whipping from side to side and she was calling out Clint's name as he fucked her so hard that they both worked up a sweat.

When her breathing started to catch in her throat and her lips tightened around his shaft, Clint slowed his pace. He gently traced his fingers down her back and moved his hips in a slow, grinding circle. He could feel the orgasm building to a climax in his as well as her body.

Valerie's breathing became quick and choppy. Her muscles tightened and she responded doubly to every little motion he made. Finally, after he waited and then pounded into her one more time, Clint felt her entire body tremble as she let out a long, passionate moan.

Speeding up just a bit, Clint gave in to what he wanted the most and just pumped into her until his own orgasm took him over. By the time he came, Valerie was barely able to hold herself up and when he finally pulled out of her, they collapsed onto the ground.

FORTY-THREE

The sun was less than halfway up when an alarm was sounded throughout the convoy of motionless wagons. It wasn't the kind of alarm that was all noise and bluster, but the kind that moved like a series of ripples over an otherwise motionless pond.

It started once the first members of a few patrols came up missing. First one had dropped off and was presumed to be following a trail of his own or even answering nature's call behind a bush somewhere. But not only did that man stay missing, but another man was unaccounted for as well.

That was when Sergeant Velasco began storming through the camp like he was ready to mount a charge. Being careful not to make enough noise that would be heard outside the camp, the bald soldier went to each wagon in turn and checked on the people inside.

For the most part, the only ones still inside the wagons were not his men. They were the ones that his men were protecting and one of them in particular was the reason for the entire convoy in the first place. Velasco studied each of those faces carefully, not offering a word of explanation as he stuck his head into each wagon and took a quick count.

The sergeant nearly went for his gun when he turned around and found himself looking into the face of the man who'd accompanied him on patrol the previous night. Biting back the reflex to draw on the private anyhow, Velasco scowled at the other man until his nerves were back in check.

"Shouldn't sneak up on an armed man, Private. That's a hell of a good way to get yourself killed."

The private's hand snapped up to the brim of his hat in a perfect, crisp salute. "Sorry, sir. I thought you'd like to know that there's another man missing, sir."

"Goddammit," Velasco snarled. "Who is it this time?"

"Adler, Sir. He didn't report back from outer patrol."

"Outer patrol? That means he could have been missing for the last four hours or so. Didn't anyone hear anything? A shot? A horse rearing? Any god damned thing at all?"

Hesitant to be the bearer of still more bad news, the private paused for a moment and then marched on ahead by responding, "No sir. Nothing at all."

Velasco nodded slowly as he thought about what he was hearing. When he noticed some curious glances coming from the inside the closest wagon, he turned on his heels and started walking away from the parked carriage. The private followed without having to be told.

"I want you to make the rounds and account for every man assigned to this detail," the sergeant ordered. "You're even to check on the ones out on patrol by riding out and getting visual confirmation of them all. You don't have to ride up and talk to them all, but I want you to exchange hand signals and I want you to set your eyes on every last man. Understand me, soldier?"

"Yes sir."

"After that, I want you to..." Sergeant Velasco's voice trailed off in mid-command. The stocky man had been pacing back and forth as he talked and froze the instant he'd turned and paced in the direction of the wagons.

For a moment, the private thought his commanding officer was just pausing to think. Then he saw the intense look in Velasco's eyes. Following the other man's line of sight, the private looked toward the nearby ground and then farther on toward the convoy.

When his eyes got to the wheels of the closest wagon, the private felt a cold grip clench around his stomach.

Sergeant Velasco was already striding over to that same wheel and didn't stop until he was close enough to reach out and run his fingers along several sets of cracked wooden spokes.

Taking his cue from Velasco, the private kept quiet even as his hand went to the gun at his side.

"I checked these wagons myself not too long ago," the sergeant whispered. "Since these wheels didn't get this way from the ride in here, that means someone broke them on purpose."

"And if you just checked them," the private added, "that means whoever broke them must still be nearby."

Velasco craned his head up slowly and looked into the other man's eyes. He'd already drawn his standard issue Colt revolver. "Call in as many of the men as you can without drawing too much attention. There's a snake crawling around here that doesn't want us to go anywhere and I'd rather not scare it off before I put a bullet through its head."

The private nodded sharply and was on his way to his horse before Velasco even had a chance to return a salute. As ordered, the younger man walked with quick steps, but didn't move in a way that gave the appearance of any kind of desperation.

Inside his head, the private was trying to keep his racing thoughts from forcing him into a misstep. When he'd been given this assignment, he was told that it was dangerous but had accepted it anyway due to the prestige of guarding the president himself.

Now, Private Henshaw wondered if volunteering to stop a bullet was worth the impressive mark on his record. That doubt lasted until he got to his horse and started riding out to the closest patrollers. In the end, it was the training that overtook his mind and body. Private Henshaw had a duty to do and he wasn't about to let himself get distracted from it.

Sergeant Velasco watched the younger man go and knew he would be all right the moment Henshaw climbed onto his saddle. Letting the other man carry out his orders, Velasco turned his attention to the more urgent business at hand.

Sure enough, it appeared that the snake had already gotten to the rest of the wagons as well. All of them had at least one broken wheel and none of them were in any condition to roll before repairs were made.

Fine then, the sergeant figured. If this snake wanted to stay and fight, a fight was exactly what he would get.

FORTY-FOUR

Sergeant Velasco's mind raced to try and think of a way to find whoever was sabotaging the wagons before any more damage was done. He didn't have to think too hard to figure out what the traitor's target was. The only problem was getting to him before the snake found a way to get to the president.

If the first objective was to keep the wagons from moving, there was only one other logical thing to do. Velasco put himself in the boots of the enemy and followed through using his own logic. If he was in the other man's place, he'd want to take care of at least some of the horses.

Sergeant Velasco took that conclusion and ran with it since time was of the essence and the life of the president of the United States hung in the balance. Shifting his eyes down low, Velasco looked for anything unusual on the ground near the horses.

Less than ten seconds later, he found exactly what he'd been looking for.

His pistol came up and he aimed at the figure he saw crawling with his belly to the ground. Whoever the man was, he was approaching the team of the guards' wagon just like the snake he was. Velasco reached out to press the end of the barrel against the other man's head.

"Hold your hands out," the sergeant said. "And make it real slow."

Adam Meers let out a slow breath and stretched out his arms just as he'd been instructed. Right before his right arm was fully extended, he reached for the little knife that had been clenched in his teeth and rolled to one side.

Reflexively, Velasco took a shot. Instead of seeing the spray of blood that he'd been expecting, he only saw a hole get punched into the ground and dirt get kicked up on impact. His eyes were already tracking the figure on the ground and his gun was moving to adjust his aim. Velasco was too late to do anything before he caught a stray beam of sunlight glinting off a sliver of metal.

Meers had been planning on using the dagger clutched in his teeth to cripple a horse or two and cause a distraction, but he could throw the blade just as well. In one fluid motion, he plucked the knife from between his teeth and flipped it through the air.

The blade was sharp enough to enter Velasco's chest like it was cutting through warm butter. Only the hilt prevented it from stabbing in any farther, but the point had gone in far enough to puncture Velasco's heart.

Meers kept rolling to the side as the horses reared up in response to the close-range gunfire. Before the sergeant's body hit the dirt, Meers was already out from under the wagon and drawing a pistol from the double rig slung over his shoulders. Drawing both guns while stopping his roll with one extended foot, the assassin aimed toward the wagon's side door just as it swung open and a pair of darkly dressed figures came out.

Although not a smart way to fire the weapons, Meers squeezed both triggers at once, sending one bullet into each of the two soldiers' chests before they could even see who'd shot them. One man took a round through the heart and dropped straight back into the coach. The other was hit in a lung and spun awkwardly out of the wagon, bouncing off the side of the carriage before dropping onto his back.

By this time, the entire camp was alive with noise and movement. There were horses thundering in from patrol and more soldiers rushing out to try and figure out what was happening. Meers used only the gun in his right hand to fire into the wagon where the other two guards had been sitting.

The other two guards still inside the wagon had had time to draw, but weren't given much of a target. Meers peeked inside just once, committed the scene to memory and then ducked back so he could just reach around and fill the inside of the coach with hot lead.

One of the guards took a bullet in the upper chest and the last man was hit in the thigh as he threw himself out of the wagon through the door on the side opposite of Meers. His reflexes had been good enough to draw his gun the moment he heard the first shot, but when he hit the ground, the pain from his leg wound sent a wave of nausea through his whole body. The edges of his vision blackened and when he blinked it clear, he saw a face staring at him from the other side and beneath the wagon.

Having already traded the empty gun in his right hand for the one in his left, Meers spotted where the fourth soldier had fallen and put a bullet directly between the guard's eyes. He didn't wait around to watch the guard die. Instead, Meers got to his feet and reloaded his pistols in quick, well-practiced motions.

He could hear plenty of other men coming. When he got to his feet, Meers snapped both pistols shut and started walking down the row of wagons. He was intent enough on his mission to ignore the pain in his leg, and the fact that it had begun bleeding. Inside, he was cursing himself for not narrowing down his focus to the exact spot where the president was hiding. He'd been able to scout a few of the wagons, but didn't know which of the remaining two was the one he wanted.

The time for scouting was over. His cover had already gone up in smoke and now was the time to dive in and get his hands dirty. The convoy wasn't going anywhere, which was a definite advantage for the assassin. He'd picked his spot and chosen his time. His hand might have been forced slightly, but Meers still had no doubt in his mind that he would be able to finish this job.

After all, there was no turning back now.

Even though he'd only been looking for a minute or so, Private Henshaw could tell that not all of the patrols were present. He knew where to look and what to look for and could only spot less than half of the riders there should have been. He didn't know where the others were and wasn't able to figure it out before he'd heard shooting coming from the camp.

Henshaw rode at full speed back that way and could still hear the report of guns being fired and men raising the alarm. When he'd gotten a little closer, he saw smoke hanging around one of the wagons and bodies lying on either side of the carriage. So far, the horses were anxious, but were trained well enough to keep from bolting.

Standing close to that same wagon, holding a gun in each hand, was a man dressed in the colors which designated him as one of the president's guards. Henshaw couldn't make out the man's face, but could see him gesturing toward the rear of the line of wagons.

Henshaw wanted to ride up and ask what had happened. He wanted to see who the man was and who was lying on the ground. But something had obviously gone very wrong and he was needed at the back of the camp. With his mind focusing on his duty, Private Henshaw steered his horse to where he was being pointed and hoped that Sergeant Velasco would be nearby to fill him in.

As soon as he was turned in the proper direction, Henshaw spotted what the other guard might have been pointing him toward. There was a dark horse coming in fast from the north like a runaway train. Not only was the horse unfamiliar, but the rider was as well. It may have been a ways off, but Henshaw could see enough of the rider's garb to know that he wasn't wearing any of the colors designed to mark the Presidential guards.

Henshaw snapped the reins of his horse, put the convoy behind him and set out directly toward the strange rider at a full gallop. His gun was at the ready and the blood raced through his veins.

Nothing was getting past him alive.

FORTY-FIVE

Clint had been riding hard for hours. Just as he'd figured, the strain was catching up to Eclipse, but the Darley Arabian stallion wasn't about to disappoint him. Foam spewed from the sides of Eclipse's mouth and his breath came in choppy, powerful bursts, but he never broke stride.

The moment he'd heard shooting in the distance, Clint had touched his heels to Eclipse's sides and gotten the stallion to dig down into his reserves and ride even faster. Clint found it hard to keep his breathing steady as he raced over the ground like he'd been shot out of a gun. Behind him, Valerie just held on for dear life.

Clint figured the assassin would try to kill the president before the wagons reached Fresno. That was simply the easiest thing to do. He only wished he'd had some way of knowing where the convoy was going to stop, so he could get there before anyone got hurt.

With the echoes of gunshots still rolling around in his head, Clint knew he was too late to prevent bloodshed. He just hoped he wasn't too late to save the president's life.

There were several horses closing in on the wagons.

Although they weren't in military uniforms, Clint didn't have much trouble picking out the bright colors of their armbands and bandannas. He ignored all of them, which wasn't hard because none of them seemed too interested in him either.

There was one rider in particular who separated from the rest. Instead of riding toward the wagons, this one was heading straight for Clint. Spotting that one immediately, Clint drew his Colt and turned to speak quickly over his shoulder.

"Keep your head down," he said to Valerie.

The brunette did just that and squeezed him just a little tighter.

Clint lined up his shot as easily as pointing his finger, but held off on pulling the trigger until he got a better look at the rider's face. A shot was fired from that man's gun and a bullet whipped past Clint's head but Clint still held back.

At the last possible second, Clint got a look at the rider's features and saw they didn't match those of Meers's face. That was all Clint had to see. Lowering the Colt, he crouched down over Eclipse's back and steered the Darley Arabian in a series of zigzagging maneuvers that were erratic enough to dodge the rest of the soldier's bullets.

By the time Clint thundered past Private Henshaw, the soldier had emptied his gun and was reaching for the rifle hanging from his saddle. The private had a hell of a time getting his horse turned around right away since Clint had passed by so closely that he'd all but knocked the soldier clean onto the ground.

There were plenty of bullets flying through the air, but unfortunately most of them were coming toward Clint. After hearing gunshots himself before, Clint couldn't figure out why everyone was more inclined to shoot at him instead of the man that had started it all.

The moment Clint circled around the wagons and got a look at the men on the other side of them, he knew exactly why he was drawing most of the fire. Dead bodies littered the ground near the wagons and blood stained the soil. For the most part, the soldiers standing in the area looked confused and anxious to fight.

Having seen the assassin before, Clint was able to pick out Meers from the rest, but only by the killer's face. Meers was dressed in the same colors as the soldiers and walked among them, taking full advantage of the confusion surrounding the wagons.

Meers had worked his way up to the second wagon in the convoy and was reaching out to take hold of the handle of the side door. "That's him!" Meers shouted. "Take him down!"

Every part of Clint's world seemed to slow down. Even as all those guns swung toward him, he saw Meers getting ready to open the door of the wagon he'd been approaching. Eclipse was about to run past that same wagon, carrying Clint through the thick of the incoming fire. Suddenly, he came up with a plan of action that seemed like the only possible way for him to have a shot at getting to Meers while also avoiding the greatest amount of incoming fire.

"What the hell are you doing?" Valerie screamed when she saw where Clint was headed.

"I'm riding straight into them."

"You're what!?"

"Too late for a discussion. No turning back."

As Clint rode toward the wagon, he put Eclipse through some jarring turns which would have caused most other horses to lose their footing. Not only did the Darley Arabian keep on all fours, but he performed the maneuvers with such precision that not one of the soldiers' bullets found their mark.

Once Clint got closer to the wagon where Meers was

standing, the incoming gunshots tapered off and stopped.
In one fluid motion, Clint swung a leg over Eclipse's back
and balanced with one foot in the stirrups. He kept his
eyes on Meers, his body moving in rhythm with Eclipse's
strides until it was time to go for broke.

Clint pushed away from the horse just as Meers pulled
the carriage door open. Hitting the ground with both feet,
Clint collapsed himself into a ball, rolled forward and
shouted the command that would bring Eclipse to a stop.

Clint came to a stop as well, sighting down the Colt's
barrel from his back lying on the ground. Less than a
heartbeat passed in actual time, but for both Clint and
Meers, that brief moment seemed to last a lot longer.

Meers had his eyes on the president and his gun was
an inch away from being lined up properly.

Clint, on the other hand, was in position and ready to
fire. He took his shot and blew a hole through the side of
Meers's skull, spilling the assassin's brains onto the carriage and the dirt at his feet.

As soon as he saw Meers drop, Clint tossed his Colt
to one side and held both hands high over his head.

"My name's Clint Adams, Mr. President. That man
was just about to kill you and I was sent to stop him."

Although dressed in a plain brown suit and a simple
hat, the president still managed to retain an air of power
and dignity as he grabbed hold of the side of the wagon
and pulled himself out. Soldiers on horseback were
swarming in on all sides and there were even several with
guns drawn inside the wagon with the president.

Before any of those men could fire another shot, the
president stopped them with a stern look and raised hand.
Once he saw that the men were obeying his order, the
president glared down at Clint who was still sprawled in
the dirt.

"How did you know I was here?" the president asked.

"I was sent by Jim West in the Secret Service. Take a

look at the man I shot. He's not one of your soldiers. He was here to kill you, sir."

The president shifted his gaze to Meers's dead, bloody face. "I'll be damned." Looking back to Clint, the president climbed down from the carriage and offered a hand to help him up. "You took one hell of a risk coming here. Not even the Service could have gotten word to us in time. You're either a hell of a patriot or one lucky, lucky man."

Dusting himself off as soon as he was back on his feet, Clint looked around at the soldiers who glared at him with suspicion still on their faces. "Actually, I'd seen Meers before and recognized his face. Beyond that, I hoped that your men would rather let me get a little closer instead of taking a chance on shooting you by mistake." Clint looked around at the bodies of the soldiers lying in the dirt and added, "I just wish I could have gotten here sooner."

"I thank you for coming at all, Mr. Adams. It's a pleasure to finally meet you. I've heard so many good things."

It didn't happen too often, but Clint was left speechless.

Watch for

BIG-SKY BANDITS

268th novel in the exciting GUNSMITH series
from Jove

Coming in April!

J. R. ROBERTS

THE GUNSMITH